WICKED AWAKENING

CLAIMED BY GARGOYLES BOOK 2

BOOK SERIES BY SARAH PIPER

M/F Romance Series

Monstrous Obsessions

Vampire Royals of New York

Reverse Harem Romance Series

Claimed by Gargoyles

The Witch's Monsters

Tarot Academy

The Witch's Rebels

GET CONNECTED!

I love connecting with readers! There are a few different ways you can keep in touch:

Email: sarah@sarahpiperbooks.com

TikTok: @sarahpiperbooks

Facebook group: Sarah Piper's Sassy Witches

Twitter: @sarahpiperbooks

Newsletter: Never miss a new release or a sale! Sign up for the VIP Readers Club: sarahpiperbooks.com/readers-club

10 Years Ago...

Despite how magic goes down in all the movies, the contents of my cauldron do *not*, in fact, boil and bubble.

They explode, splattering me and Mrs. Larkum in sticky blue goo.

Not too hot, not too cold, not too toxic... Just freaking mortifying.

"Oh, Westlyn." My teacher frowns beneath the mess dripping down her face, clearly disappointed. I swear the woman has never encountered a witch who couldn't master the fine art of potions and charms under her expert tutelage, but here I go, blazing trails again.

"I'm doing everything in my power to help you," she continues, reaching for a tissue, "but I can't force the spells and correspondences into your mind. If you want to pass my class, you're going to have to do more than just stay after school. You need to develop a positive mindset, put in the work, and meet me halfway."

"I'm trying—honestly." I drag my sleeve across my face, wiping the goo from my eyes. "But I'm never going to be able to cast these spells. That's not a negative mindset—it's just a fact. I've got no magic of my own."

"No, but you still need to learn the material. One day, if destiny is kind, you'll marry into a mage family, where you'll be expected to support your partner in all things magical and mundane. You can't be an asset to them if you don't know your silver slipper powder from your essence of nightwing."

I wipe my eyes again, grateful for the excuse to cover my face, which is definitely scowling now.

Marry into a mage family... Be an asset...

Right.

For a witch with no mojo, that's as big as my dreams and aspirations are allowed to get.

I've accepted that. But all the forced positivity in the world won't make me happy about it.

By the time we clean up the classroom and put away the supplies, it's already dark outside, the deep autumn shadows of Manhattan coming alive beneath the city lights.

"Goodness, I didn't realize how late it was." Mrs. Larkum grabs her coat and hits the classroom lights. "Do you need me to call you a cab?"

"No, my dad's picking me up." I force the lie through a too-bright smile. "He's taking me out for dim sum."

"That sounds nice. Well, in the meantime, keep striving, Westlyn. It's not time to give up on yourself just yet."

Goddess. I know she means well, but all I want to say is, *so when is it time? Will you let me know, so I can put it on the calendar?*

Anyway, I don't want to disappoint her any more than I already have, so I do the expected thing, as usual—lock in that positive mindset smile, promise I'll keep trying, and follow her out into the street.

I'm still smiling as we say our goodbyes and I walk alone past Skyline Laundromat and Big Belly Burrito.

Still smiling when I turn the corner at Cheng's grocer and wave to Mr. Cheng, who's busy sticking plastic-wrapped bouquets into buckets outside the storefront.

And still smiling on my way to the train… right up until the part where my fellow magical academy student and undisputed champion douchebag Jacob Pomeroy steps out of the alley between a boarded-up hair salon and a hipster brunch place, hands in his pockets, smirk twisting his evil face.

My throat closes up. I nearly trip in my haste to get away, but it's no use.

"Look who it is, boys," he sneers, stepping so far into my personal space I can smell the cheap booze on his breath. "Wicked Westlyn."

"And she's smiling!" This from Alonzo Florentine, Jake's

partner in crime. He crowds in close, too. Tugs on one of my braids. "What's so funny, Wicked? Care to share with the class?"

"Fuck off." I swat his hand away, but he comes right back for another grab, this time touching some of the left-overs from my failed spell. "Looks like you tried to give Papa Smurf a blowjob and missed."

"Smurf fucker!" A peal of laughter sounds from the alley, and another guy slinks out—a dude everyone calls Full Metal Jacket on account of how completely insane he is. I don't even know his real name, but he certainly knows mine. "Wicked Westlyn, wandering the city streets alone. It'd be a real shame if anything happened to you."

"Not like anyone would miss her," Alonzo says, the three of them now circling me like hungry raptors. "Just a useless, impotent witch taking up space."

Behind me, Jake grabs my hips and thrusts against my ass. "Too bad you're tainted, or I'd show you what you're missing out on. Papa Smurf ain't got nothing on me."

I try to jerk free, but he's relentless, holding me in place while his friends tug and poke, leer and mock.

A few people pass by on the sidewalk, but no one pays us any mind. Just a couple of kids messing around, they assume. Nothing to see here, move along...

"I heard witches without magic come from hell," Alonzo says. "Demons steal your magic while you're still in the womb."

"Her mother died," Metal says. "Probably fucked too many demons."

Tears well in my eyes, but I refuse to let them fall. My bullies have already stolen enough from me this semester. I won't give them the satisfaction.

"Aww, what's wrong, wicked little beast?" Jake mocks, his breath hot and sour on the back of my neck. "No more smiles?"

Alonzo grabs my face, squeezing so hard my teeth cut the insides of my cheeks. Then he smashes his mouth into mine and shoves his tongue inside me, laughing the entire time.

When he finally pulls back, he's still laughing. "Come on, Wicked. We're just playing. Don't hex us or—oh, wait! That's right! You can't!"

More raucous laughter.

"Too bad they don't make Viagra for witches." Metal grabs his crotch and wags his tongue at me. "You need a dick for that."

"Guess you can't use it either, then," I finally retort, spitting the taste of Alonzo out of my mouth.

Stupid. I know better than to taunt mage boys, especially when they're traveling in packs, but the words are out before I can stop them.

"Oh, I've got a dick, bitch. I'd show it to you, but I'm not sure you'd know what to do with it."

"Do *you*?" I snap, again with the ill-timed mouth.

He unzips his pants and shoves a hand down his boxers. "You wanna find out?"

"Maybe some other time." I roll my eyes and feign indifference, praying to the goddess I can keep my simmering fear in check. Mage boys can smell it a mile off. "Anyway, my dad's waiting for me up the block, so—"

"Waiting at the blackjack table, more likely." Jake slides his arm around my waist and hauls me back against his chest. "Waiting for his ship to come in. Too bad it's never gonna happen. 'Loser' runs in your family."

"I heard he tried to sell you on Craigslist," Alonzo says, "but the only offers he got were from pimps."

"Not even a pimp would pay money for *this* magicless whore." Metal shoves his hand between my thighs and gives me a hard squeeze through my jeans. Then, in a dark whisper, "But lucky for us, we get you for free. And now we're gonna fuck a little magic back into your soul. Would you like that?"

My fear turns into a full-on panic. My hands and feet turn hot and prickly, my heart slamming inside my ribs.

"Let me go," I grind out, but this only eggs them on. Jake tightens his hold, the other two quickly looking around as if they're confirming there aren't any witnesses.

No. No, no, no!

I suck in a breath to scream for help, but Jake's clamping his hand over my mouth.

Let me go, let me go, let me go...

The words scroll through my mind like a spell, and I squeeze my eyes shut, begging the goddess to let this work. This stupid, simple distraction magic—just this one time. This one fucking time, let me not be a failure...

I frantically try to remember Mrs. Larkum's lectures on spell casting... Picture the desired outcome, hold the image in mind...

A cop, a mother, a gangbanger, anyone *passing by the alley and shooing the boys away...*

But no one comes.

The boys don't scatter.

And now they're all around me, big mouths taunting me, big hands dragging me into the alley, back behind the dumpster. I try to kick free, try to scream, but they're too strong, too cruel, too everything...

They're going to rape me. They're going to rape and mutilate me and leave my broken body bleeding out in the alley and my father won't even know I'm dead...

Fear sours my gut, and with one last surge of pure adrenaline, I slam my head backward and stomp down hard, simultaneously smashing Jake's nose and crushing his instep. With a howl of pain, he shoves me away and stumbles back, but I still can't escape. The other guys are on me again in a blink, smothering my screams, stealing my breath, dragging me down, down, down...

"Stop wiggling, whore." Metal straddles me on the ground and pins my wrists over my head, the concrete scraping my skin raw. Alonzo holds my feet, and then out of nowhere, Jake's back. He kneels beside me, broken nose leaking blood into his mouth, a flash of something silver in his hand—a pen? A knife?—and then he grabs my throat and jabs me hard in the neck and everything just... goes... dark.

CHAPTER TWO

WESTLYN

10 Years Ago...

Oil. Some kind of motor oil. Rotten garbage. Piss. A dead rodent and the unmistakable scent of lit candles...

The discordant mix assaults my nose, making me gag. I gasp for breath, and my eyelids fly open, awareness rushing through me in a hot wave.

I'm lying face-down on the subway tracks, spread eagle, bound to the rails by my wrists and ankles. Black candles surround me, their flickering yellow-orange glow the only light source in the tunnel.

I'm naked from the waist up.

My jeans, thankfully, are still intact, and I don't feel any pain down there.

But my relief at the small miracle is short-lived, fear flooding my limbs with a vengeance.

"Good morning, wicked little beast," the dark voice taunts. "Enjoy the nap?"

Jake.

He and his boys emerge from the tunnel with several others I recognize from school, the candlelight exaggerating their features, making them look even more vicious and terrifying than they did aboveground.

"Help!" I scream, not wasting my chance this time. I remember learning that you're supposed to yell 'fire' when you need help because people are more likely to respond. So that's what I do. "Fire! Fire! Somebody help!"

My pleas echo down the endless tunnel behind them. I whip my head around, frantically trying to get my bearings, desperate to find a friendly face.

There aren't any, though. Only monsters.

"Scream all you want, Wicked," Metal says. "No one will hear you. No one will come."

"That's... that's not true," I stammer. "The police are always..."

The words die on my tongue as the realization hits.

This is an abandoned station.

The subway platform is empty. Nothing but chipped tiles and rusted metal beams as far as the eye can see. Old newspapers and trash strewn across the concrete. A cracked sign indicating the train lines—four, five, six.

But just because it's not an active subway stop doesn't mean the trains skip over it.

Fresh panic seizes my chest.

"Untie me!" I shout, my throat cracking with the effort. "The trains still pass through here!"

"The four train, yep," Metal says. "Doesn't stop, though. Doesn't even slow down." He glances at his phone. "But we've got an hour before the next one's due, which gives us *plenty* of time."

"T-time for what?" I ask. Tears run down my cheeks, mixing with snot.

"Since a demon fucked your mother and stole your magic," Jake says, "we're gonna do you a favor and conjure your demon daddy. See if he might give you back your mojo."

"Let me go!" I beg, way more terrified about the train than I am about them actually being able to summon a demon. These assholes have been bullying me all semester, but they've never taken it this far before. "Please! This isn't funny anymore. Quit fucking around and let me go!"

But Alonzo's already pouring salt on the tracks, casting me in a ritual circle, and Jake's pulling a spellbook and some kind of athame out of his backpack.

Candlelight glints off the curved blade. It's about six inches long, the metal etched with shadow mage symbols.

Stolen from his parents, most likely. Kids our age aren't allowed to have ritual tools like that—not even shadow mages, who basically run the magical world around here.

"Time to spill a little blood for the demons, boys." He grins at me, and I can tell from the sick gleam in his eyes he's not talking about *their* blood.

He's talking about mine.

"Don't," I say. It's barely a whisper, my lips trembling.

"*Do*." His smile drops away, the insanity in his eyes chilling me to the core. "Showtime."

He kneels beside me, the other boys crowding in to join him. I don't know who's pinching me, who's spitting on me, who's laughing—they're all around me now, all a blur.

I try to close my eyes, but Metal fists my hair. "No sleeping on the job, Wicked. We need you conscious and alert for this."

"Fuck you," I hiss.

He smashes my face into the muck between the tracks, then yanks my head up again to meet his eyes. "No thanks, whore. Now hold still."

"I offer this blood," Jake calls out, his voice firm and commanding as it echoes through the tunnel, "in service to the demons from whence it spawned."

The blade touches my back, a brief shock of ice-cold metal, and then...

No...

The first cut is like fire, the blade tearing through my flesh, blood trickling hot down my side. The second is even worse, deep and slow and murderous.

Everything inside me trembles. I puke until there's nothing left in my stomach but bile.

And then I scream.

I scream through all of it.

Through the laughter and rough hands and taunts.

Through all the cuts that come after, a mad flurry of slashes and stabs and hot blood spilling onto the tracks.

"Wicked Westlyn," Jake whispers. "We all know you're a wicked little whore. Now, everyone else will know, too."

"Wicked Westlyn," the others join in, their cruel chants becoming the soundtrack of my torture.

The pain is endless. Stars dance before my eyes. My heart feels like it's going to explode.

And all the while, the boys keep chanting, alternating between "Wicked Westlyn" and some botched demonic summoning spell.

The tunnel spins in the darkness. I can't feel my arms or legs.

I can barely remember my own name.

Suddenly the chanting stops and Alonzo goes, "Dude, I gotta take a leak."

"Be my guest," Jake says, and they all get to their feet and step away from me.

I blow out a deep breath, grateful for the momentary reprieve from that vicious blade and Metal's cruel hands in my hair.

But then they're laughing again, and Alonzo's unzipping his pants, and before I even realize what's happening, he's pissing on me.

My back is on fire again.

I want to disappear.

"Please," I gasp, one last time. "You had your fun, okay? Just let me—"

A bright light illuminates the tunnel at the bend, stealing my words and kicking my heart back into overdrive.

"Dude!" Metal shouts. "Train!"

"It's early!" Alonzo tucks his dick away, then they're all shouting at each other, scrambling to grab their bags from the tracks.

"Get her up!" Jake yells, and someone makes a half-assed attempt to untie me, but it doesn't work and I can't tell what's going on and they're all yelling and then they're leaving and...

"Wait!" I shout, drawing on the last of my strength and tugging viciously on the binds, but it's no use. They're so tight, the rope is cutting into my skin. "Don't leave me like this! Cut the ropes! Cut the fucking ropes!"

But they don't. They're already back up on the platform above me, shoving each other, fighting. I hear the words "murder" and "prison." Jake shouts something like, "We were supposed to keep her alive!" and Metal says, "Fuck this. It's not even worth the money," and then the train is on the straightaway barreling toward the station, the force of the air ahead of it extinguishing most of the candles.

Sobbing, I press my cheek into the sickness and muck, squeeze my eyes shut tight, and send another desperate prayer to the goddess, to the devil, to the demons they couldn't summon, to *anyone* in this realm or the next who might hear my pleas...

I don't want to die I don't want to die I don't want to die...

The sound of the approaching train is deafening.

The boys are long gone.

They brutalized me. Tortured me. And then they left me here, injured and bleeding and humiliated.

A dark realization sweeps over me, and I know with utter certainty—as I lay here shivering and sobbing in the darkness, covered in blood and piss and filth—this is the place where I'm going to die.

CHAPTER THREE

DRAEGAN

It's only been a few hours since we got things sorted with the fire inspector on the Forsythe blaze, and despite my best efforts to wrap up my evening in peace with a nice, hot cuppa from Stella's café, it seems fate is determined to ruin it for me.

Tonight's particular ruination comes in the form of an ambush by my dear friend, Detective *fucking* Reedsy.

Bloody hell. I've been in the city all night dealing with bullshit urban planning officials and zoning restrictions and then the damn fire inspector, and now, all I want to do is pick up my tea, hit the skies, and get back to the manor without incident. Jude and Rook left right after our meeting, which leaves plenty of time for Jude to get into trouble. I'm *fairly* certain he was only bluffing when he threatened to turn the inspector's torso into a footrest, but when it comes to my enforcer's antics of late, we can't be too careful.

Unfortunately, dealing with Reedsy means leaving Jude unsupervised a bit longer.

"Good evening, detective." I give him the briefest nod as I open the café door and gesture him inside. "Out for a late-night coffee run?"

Unmoving, Reedsy shakes his head, eyes glimmering with his usual disdain, the scent of whiskey heavy on his breath. Through a fake smile, he says, "A moment of your time, Caldwell? If you don't mind."

"Actually, I do mind. I need to—"

"It wasn't really a request."

I release the door and fold my arms across my chest, the gargoyle beneath my glamour stirring. "Have you been waiting all night for me?"

"Figured you'd show up eventually. Stella's is practically your second home."

"So you're following me. Wonderful. Well, let's get on with it, then. Do I need a lawyer present?"

"Nah. It's just a few questions between old pals."

"Isn't it always," I grumble.

He takes out his notepad and flips it open, as if he can't remember his own lines in our ridiculous charade. "What can you tell me about the fire at Lennon and Celine Forsythe's home?"

"Fire?" I press my hand to my chest, feigning concern. "Goodness, is everyone all right?"

"Don't play dumb with me, Caldwell. Just answer the question."

"I assure you, detective, this is the first I've heard of it."

He rolls his glassy eyes. "Really. You mean to tell me you *weren't* harassing the fire inspector earlier tonight?"

"Harassing?" I laugh. "Well, if *that's* how the inspector is categorizing our visits, perhaps I need to up my hospitality game. Do you think he's fond of pastries? Maybe some nice, fresh muffins. Oh! Or those cinnamon chocolate croissants with the little frosted—"

"So you admit you were there tonight?"

"The bakery?"

"The inspector's *office*, Caldwell."

"Oh, right. Forgive me. Brain's a little foggy on account of the unexpected delay in caffeine consumption. Anyway, yes, I was there. Along with my associates, Jude Hendrix and Rook Van Doren. We had a meeting on another matter."

"*What* other matter?"

"That's of a proprietary business nature. I'm afraid I can't disclose—"

"You can either disclose it, or you can accompany me uptown to the precinct, where I'll tie you up in red tape and paperwork until the morning, and force you to disclose it then."

He smiles, knowing he's bested me, but clueless about the reason why. If I could, I'd wait him out for days, enjoying every second of making him look foolish. But sunrise and gargoyles don't exactly mix, and I'm not sure the good ol' boys in blue uptown are quite ready to see a man turn into a stone gargoyle before their very eyes.

So, grinning and bearing it, I say, "Blackmoor Capital owns a great many old buildings in this city, detective. Most of which require extensive upgrades for fire safety and other building code issues. Meeting with the fire inspector is a somewhat regular occurrence for us. You're welcome to join in some time—perhaps you'll learn something about this city you're tasked with protecting and serving. Now, I've a very busy schedule, so if there's nothing else—"

"There's *plenty* else, Caldwell. Plenty else." He gets right in my face, jabbing a finger into my chest. "One of these days, you're going to drop your guard and make a mistake. And that's when I'll finally swoop in and nail you to the wall, and trust me when I tell you I'm gonna fuck you so hard, your goddamn *descendants* will still be walking with a limp."

"Or maybe," I say softly, flashing him the kind of grin that would make Jude proud, "I'll bring those cinnamon-chocolate pastries to *your* goddamn descendants, along with my condolences over the mysterious disappearance of their father, whose body was never found. Always such a shame when an upstanding officer of the law vanishes in the line of duty, especially when he leaves a family behind. What a fucking tragedy."

His face pales, and he finally lowers his finger.

In the deadly silence that follows, I offer one last cordial smile. "Farewell, detective. Feel free to give me a ring if you've got any more questions. You know I *always* look forward to our little chats. Oh, and my best to the wife and kids."

I leave him to do whatever it is crooked cops do when they've just been threatened by their favorite suspects, and head back to my office. No time for tea now, thanks to Reedsy's annoying intrusion, but perhaps there's a silver lining in this storm cloud after all.

Reedsy's questioning about the fire has just given me the perfect opportunity to put the Archmage *more* solidly on my shit list, and *less* solidly on our trail, hopefully buying us a bit of breathing room with his most coveted treasures— Westlyn Avery and the Cerridwen Codex.

Time to pick up the phone... and pick a fight with my favorite shadow mage.

It takes three separate calls before the prick finally answers, and when he does, I don't give him the opportunity to speak so much as a hello.

"I've just missed my evening tea, Lennon. Care to know why? Because Detective Reedsy has taken to assaulting me in the street on your behalf."

"Draegan, this isn't a good time. I—"

"First you accuse me—behind my back, I might add—of being involved in the disappearance of your son's runaway bride. Just when I think we've moved past that, I'm questioned in the street like some sort of arsonist? Honestly, Lennon. I really believed we were building something here. If not a friendship, an alliance at the very least."

"There's no need to get upset. I merely—"

"Upset? *Upset?* I'm bloody *livid.* Your underhandedness during our last visit is what's spurring him on. Now, my reputation is being called into question right out in public, and if you think for one *moment* I appreciate that, you'd better consult your crystal ball or Tarot cards or whatever divination method has so clearly led you astray, and ask again."

"I apologize for the detective's assertiveness, Draegan, but you must understand—"

"Oh, I *do* understand. I understand you need to get your house in order and stop sending the dogs after your so-called allies. Now, as relieved as I was to hear no one was hurt during the fire, I have one *very* important concern." Taking a page out of Westlyn's playbook on dramatics, I unleash a put-upon sigh. "*Please* tell me the Cerridwen Codex was tucked away at an offsite location and is not currently a pile of ashes."

It's what he'd expect me to care about, after all. Despite the pleasantries we've exchanged over these past several weeks, we both know our relationship isn't based on anything genuine. Just a mutual desire for power obtained by any means necessary.

It's a long moment before he answers, his breath heavy

on the other end. I can practically hear the gears of his mind whirring, weighing how much he should reveal to me.

When he finally speaks again, his voice is strained. "The Codex is gone, Draegan."

Really? You don't say…

"For fuck's sake," I grumble. "Is *any* of it salvageable? Have you consulted a restoration specialist? Fire damage can occasionally be reversed with—"

"It wasn't destroyed by the fire."

"But… I don't understand. You just said it was gone."

"Draegan," he snaps, and apparently the old man just found his balls again, because the next thing out of his mouth is, "What *I* don't understand is why you're troubling me after I just lost my home and a great many valuable artifacts under suspicious circumstances. Now, I'm sorry Reedsy has it out for you, but that's between the two of you. I've got my own problems to deal with—getting my house in order, as you've just so *compassionately* reminded me." His ire fades into a scoff. "Honestly, Draegan. Why are you so damned fixated on this random book?"

"Because it isn't just a random book, Lennon. It's part of our legacy as fae. *Ours*, not yours. Not Celine's. Not the shadow magic society's. It's a fae treasure that never should have come to you in the first place."

"You knew of my interest in fae culture. You encouraged—"

"I *indulged*, merely out of respect for what I thought was the start of a mutually beneficial alliance between our organizations and between you and me as individuals. But truthfully, your obsession with my people is shameful and appropriative, and it's—"

"I paid top dollar for that Codex! It's mine by rights!"

"You paid for it, yes. And now you're grieving its loss as a unique and valuable score—something to brag about to your fellow mages. But *I'm* grieving it as a piece of my family's legacy—a legacy that's fading all-too-quickly from the collective memory. So forgive me if I'm not as sensitive to your plight as you'd like, but I'd appreciate a bit of sensitivity on your end, too. A modicum of cultural awareness wouldn't hurt, either."

"Awareness?" He scoffs again. "I'm *quite* aware, thank you very much. Aware that you and your fae partners think you're better than the rest of us, looking down from atop your high tower in Manhattan... Preposterous."

"A bit hard to look down on you when you and your shadow mages are looking down from the same heights."

"You have *no* idea the pressure I'm under, Draegan. Not only are Celine and I dealing with this fire, but we still haven't located my future daughter-in-law *or* her parents. Hunter is just beside himself with worry. Beside himself!"

I'm grateful I made the call from the privacy of my office, because while I can volley personal insults with the man all night, the moment he mentions Westlyn, all bets are off. My protective instincts kick in hard, fury shattering my glamour and shuddering through my wings.

Yes, I'm sure Hunter-slash-Zorakkov was downright inconsolable *when your mage lackey tried to kidnap her from the restaurant, you vile filth...*

"I'm... sorry for your family troubles," I manage, my jaw aching from how tightly I'm clenching it, "but the Codex is still my primary concern. You claim it didn't burn in the fire —fine. What the hell happened to it?"

"Someone stole it, Draegan," he says, exhaustion finally chasing the indignation from his tone. "*That's* what happened to it. All that time Celine and I spent tracking it down, all that money... Now it's just gone. What a waste."

"Are you certain it was taken?"

"My entire library was destroyed," he says. "The fire department confirmed the bulk of the damage happened before the fire began. It was clearly an act of vandalism and thievery. Several important artifacts and texts seem to be missing, though we haven't been able to do a full reckoning on account of the damage—the third floor is too unstable."

Forcing a note of hope into my voice, I say, "So there's a chance the Codex is still there?"

"No. It's definitely gone. The book had certain... energetic markers. The moment we returned to the brownstone after the fire, I could sense its absence."

"But not its new location?"

"Unfortunately, no."

I let out a string of curses for his benefit, making a mental note to tell Rook about these energetic markers. I have no idea if Lennon's referring to the same sorts of things Rook and Westlyn are experiencing in the book's presence—headaches, electrical jolts—or if it's something more akin to an aftermarket mage security feature, but the last thing we need is Forsythe tracking it to the manor on account of some magical homing device we all overlooked.

"So the thief stole your artifacts," I say, "then what? Burned the evidence?"

"That's my theory. The fire inspector said the blaze was due to faulty wiring, but I know in my gut it was arson."

"Given the robbery and vandalism," I say, wondering what Westlyn would think of my acting skills, "I tend to agree with you. I don't suppose you've any leads? Other than me, of course?"

"Not yet. But my thought is... Whoever stole the Codex and set the fire is most likely the same person—or persons, if we're dealing with a cult or a rogue coven of some sort—who has Westlyn Avery."

Well, well, well. Aren't you a clever chap...

"So you're thinking if you locate one, you'll likely find the other," I say, fishing to see if he knows more than he's let on so far.

"As of now, I'm afraid I haven't been able to find either. We've got our best mages on it, but the trail's gone completely cold."

"That's... unfortunate." I blow out another breath. "Well, I'm not sure I can be much help at this point, but if I hear anything about the girl or the Codex, I'll be in touch."

"I appreciate that, Draegan. Despite our differences, I

do value our relationship. I regret that things took a turn. I... I truly hope we can find our way back to that alliance."

"Given your obvious lack of trust in me, I'm not sure that's possible. But..." I make him wait an eternity, then finally say, "Locate the lost Codex and return it to its rightful fae owners, and *then* we'll see about repairing our broken bonds."

CHAPTER FOUR

WESTLYN

I've never said the words out loud before. Never given voice to this story—my most private, horrific shame. And now that those words are out, they're just... *here*. Lingering in the stunned silence between Jude and Auggie, as dark and heavy as the air before a thunderstorm.

Last night in the library, Auggie told me that stories are bridges. "Once you know someone's stories," he said, "the deepest, darkest ones that rock us to the core and shape who we become, you're connected to that person in a way you can't undo. Even if you have a falling out, even if you never speak again after that moment, you'll always have that piece of them."

Never has that been more true for me than it is right now. And no matter what happens between us—whether I'm a part of their lives for the long haul or gone in a month —this moment, this bridge will always connect us.

The thought is as terrifying as it is comforting.

I'm still kneeling on Auggie's bed, naked but for the sweatshirt balled up in my hands, my heart pounding, tears painting my cheeks. Jude hasn't moved from his spot beside the bed, hasn't uttered a word since he demanded to know who carved the shameful word into my skin.

WICKED...

I don't think he's even drawn a single breath since I began talking. He won't meet my eyes. Neither of the gargoyles will.

None of us seem to know what's supposed to happen next.

I close my eyes, suddenly wishing Rook or Draegan would barge in. I'd take one of Rook's scientific discoveries or even one of Draegan's control-freak outbursts over this uncomfortable tension any night of the week.

But then, after what feels like a hundred years, the silence is finally broken.

"But you didn't."

It's Auggie. No more than a whisper, but I'm grateful for it anyway.

I open my eyes. Look into his warm hazel ones.

Shock and sadness have drained the color from his cheeks, his gray skin flat and lifeless.

"You said you knew that's where you were going to die," he continues. "But you didn't. You're still here. You survived."

"Thanks to some unexpected new friends." At this, I

finally manage a smile. "That was the night I met Lucinda, Huxley, and Jean-Pierre."

"The ravens," he says, his voice soft with wonder, and I nod.

"I have no idea how or why they found me—it's not like ravens make a habit of hanging out in the subway tunnels. But just when I was about to give up all hope... Suddenly, there they were, swooping down from the platform and onto the tracks. I don't know how it all happened so fast, how they weren't scared off by the train. They started going crazy, pecking at the ropes—I jerked and tugged until one hand finally tore free, then I frantically untied the other one while the birds attacked the ropes around my ankles. It worked—I was finally free. But the train... it was *right* there." I shiver as the memory rattles through me all over again. "With every bit of strength I could muster, I threw myself sideways off the tracks, smashing myself against the tunnel wall. I had just enough time to cover my head, then the train just... it roared right past me, not even slowing down."

Goddess, remembering it now... I still can't believe I survived it. Waiting for that monstrous machine to pass was the longest fifteen seconds of my life. It screeched along the tracks, hot metal mere inches from my bleeding skin... I didn't move a muscle. I just kept thinking that same thing over and over again—*I don't want to die, I don't want to die.*

But then, almost as soon as it began, it was over. The

train disappeared into the darkness, bathing me in silence once more.

"Slowly, I sat up," I tell them. "I was shaking and terrified and burning from head to toe, but I was still alive. A single candle remained lit beside me, and I remember being so grateful for it—that tiny flicker of light. I could hear my heartbeat pounding in my ears. The soft sounds of my broken sobs. The scratch and squeak of rodents scurrying back onto the tracks."

"Fuck," Auggie says. "You must've been so scared."

"I was. But I was alive, and somehow, I realized the worst of it was over. The ravens were alive, too, right by my side. And they stayed by my side as I dragged myself up onto the platform. I had no idea where I was or how to get out—it was almost pitch black in there, save for the candle I brought with me. But the birds seemed to know where they were going, so I followed them. Half my clothes were gone, but I found my backpack and jacket on the platform —the boys must've tossed them aside when they dragged me down there. I put on the jacket, followed the birds to a concrete stairwell at the other end of the station, and made my way out. I had to walk home—they stole my wallet and MetroCard—but the ravens stayed with me all the way back to Brooklyn, flying just overhead. We've been friends ever since."

"Did you go to the police?" Auggie asks.

"No point. The police would've asked too many questions, and those boys?" I shake my head, the old rage simmering. "Shadow magic society members are untouchable. Ratting them out would've been signing my own death warrant."

"What about your father?"

"Nope. He never even came home that night—probably passed out in some casino. I did what I could to clean up, found some old healing balm and bandages in the medicine cabinet. I didn't bother going back to that school—I couldn't face those boys again. When the school finally caught up with my dad, he told them I'd transferred and he forgot to put in the paperwork. Next thing I knew, I was enrolled at a new school. And then another one after that, and another one. We never talked about why—he never even asked me why I stopped going to classes. Never asked about bullying even though all the signs were there in blazing neon lights."

I close my eyes to keep the new flood of memories at bay as I tell them the rest. How I hated school. All of them. Because even though the kids' names changed, their hearts never did.

No matter where I went, I was always the weird girl who talked to birds at recess. The witch with no magic who couldn't cast a single spell. The girl whose mage father gambled away their money and flushed his reputation down the toilet.

The bullying just got worse and worse, because older kids were more clever than Jake and his crew—they knew how to hurt me without leaving permanent marks. How to say just the right things to keep me living in constant fear of retaliation... or worse.

"My father knew I was in trouble," I continue, "but he never brought it up. Never cared enough for a single conversation—not the first time I came home from school crying, and not the last. That night on the tracks? *Goddess*, I was so young. I hadn't even turned thirteen yet. Alonzo was my first kiss."

"*Fuck*," Jude breathes, the first sound he's uttered since I started us trekking down this dark path.

I glance up at him again, and this time, he doesn't look away. He's watching me closely, his cobalt blue eyes rimmed in red, burning right through me.

He's not shouting. Not smashing things. Not vowing vengeance.

Yet I've never seen him so completely undone.

Not even when he tortured and killed Randall, the fake-waiter mage who tried to kidnap me from Carmine's.

Now, towering over me beside the bed, his eyes blazing with that unspoken fury, his every cell is practically humming with the need to commit violence. I can *feel* it.

I wait for him to unleash his special brand of hell. To smash through the window, fly out into the night, and hunt down those monsters where they sleep.

But he just swallows hard. Closes his eyes. Takes a few deep, slow breaths. I can practically see that violence rippling through him from horns to wings to tail, and then... it's just gone.

When he looks at me again, there's only sadness in his eyes. Compassion. "Everything's going to be okay, little scarecrow," he whispers. "I promise."

I didn't even realize how badly I needed to hear it. Coming from him, it means everything to me.

And when my brutal, overprotective, crazy gargoyle offers a gentle smile and holds out his hand, he damn near melts my heart.

"Come on," he says. "Let's get cleaned up. You too, Augs. No one likes a crusty—"

"Always right there with the on-point visuals," he says. "Good looking out, Jude."

An unexpected laugh bubbles out of me, and I drop the sweatshirt and go to Jude, letting him wrap me up in his arms, no longer worried about the scars or the stories or the old heartbreak. Right now, all that matters is this. Us.

Jude carries me into Auggie's bathroom, his movements so smooth and graceful I feel like we're floating.

Auggie turns on the shower—a massive black marble and frosted glass affair with dual shower heads and plenty of space for everyone, gargoyle wings included. As soon as the water's hot, the three of us step inside.

Wordlessly, Auggie removes one of the handheld shower heads, and Jude grabs the soap, and with an almost reverent touch, the gargoyles who so thoroughly ravished me an hour ago finally wash me clean.

Everything inside me still aches with the burn of all the naughty, delicious things the three of us did tonight—first times for me in so many ways—yet my heart feels light and happy.

No, telling that story didn't magically erase my scars or the pain of those brutal memories. But the sour, red-hot shame I've been carrying around with them?

Tonight, I'm finally allowing myself to set it down.

The only ones who deserve to carry the shame of what happened to me are my attackers. I'm fucking done doing it for them.

And I have Jude and Augustine to thank for it. Because they listened to me as I cried, naked and afraid and trembling in that bed, and instead of making me feel weak or disgusting or helpless or downright ignored, they made me feel safe and cared for. Cherished.

Lust? That's the easy part, and it came fast and furious with us.

But a genuine feeling of safety? Of trust? Of letting someone see the darkest parts of you and knowing they've still got your back?

That feeling isn't something I take lightly.

It isn't something I've ever even felt before.

"What are you thinking, witchling?" Auggie asks, pressing a kiss to my bare shoulder. "You're a million miles away."

"No, I'm actually right here." I smile, fresh tears mixing with the hot water streaming down my cheeks. "I was thinking how crazy it is that I'm standing here completely naked, surrounded by two men who could shatter every bone in my body before I even heard the first snap, and yet—"

"No." Jude squeezes my hip. "Don't even say it. Don't *think* it. Put that right the fuck out of your mind, because Auggie and I would rather kill each other than cause you even a moment's pain."

"I'd kill him just for the fun of it," Auggie says, "but the point remains."

"Good thing you're both immortal." I laugh, then reach for them both, squeezing their hands. "I was just going to say... Even though I barely know you and you're both these big, powerful beasts, I... I've never felt so safe in my life."

Auggie cups my face. "You never have to be afraid of us, West. We will *always* protect you."

Jude says nothing, as if my confession has momentarily stolen his words, but that's okay. For now, we don't need any more.

My two gargoyles huddle in close, arms and wings wrapping around me, cocooning me in their warm embrace until the water finally runs cold and the very last vestiges of that old shame swirl away down the drain.

CHAPTER FIVE

AUGUSTINE

After Jude changes the sheets, we tuck our little witchling into my bed, her damp hair curling into black and silver ringlets, skin fresh and pink from the shower, everything about her looking sweet and serene and utterly at peace.

Moonlight streams through the window and touches her bare shoulders, and part of me is itching to grab my camera. To capture her just like this, beautiful and content and safe.

But I can't take her picture tonight. Because as much as I'm trying to keep up a brave face on the outside, here on the inside? My heart is fucking *shredded*.

Looking at her now, it's impossible to imagine anyone wanting to hurt her. To pluck so much as a single hair from her head, let alone torture her the way those fucking boys did. Just hearing her tell the story has me utterly fucking *sick* over it; one look at Jude, his jaw tight, his eyes blazing behind the thin veneer of calm, and I know he feels the same way.

He set it aside earlier because he knew she needed him to be there for her. To hold her. To tell her it would be okay.

But now, all that rage is starting to bubble up again, seeping out through the cracks. His claws are itching to tear out throats, his fangs burning with the need to devour.

I know it, because I'm right there with him.

Normally, I try to keep him in check. Balance out his worst impulses and keep us out of trouble with the law *and* with Drae.

But now? Whatever his chosen methods of torture are on this one—however vicious and messy he wants things to get—I'm fucking *down*.

Those motherfuckers don't deserve to exist in the same realm as Westlyn Avery, and we're damn well going to make sure they don't.

But first, we're going to make sure they *bleed*.

"I can barely keep my eyes open," West says softly, gazing up at me with a sleepy smile. "Two hot gargoyles can really wear a girl out. Who knew?"

"It's the sort of thing you have to discover for yourself." I laugh, kneeling on the floor beside the bed and stroking her hair. "I'll leave some bottled water for you on the nightstand in case you get thirsty."

"Thank you." Still smiling, she reaches up to touch my

face, then reaches for Jude's hand on the other side. "Both of you."

"What for, witchling?"

"For taking such good care of me, and for just... I don't know. Listening. I... I've never told anyone about all that stuff."

"No one?" I ask. "Not even Draegan?"

West shakes her head. "It's not that I'm trying to keep it a secret—well, not anymore. It's just... Okay, Rook is basically the sweetest guy ever, so I'm not worried about him. But Draegan... Well, he's pretty... intense. The two of us are oil and water on a *good* day, and I guess I just don't want him to get all weird on me because of my past."

"What do you mean, weird?" I ask.

"Some people look at you differently when they hear a story like this. Like you're broken or something."

Jude sits on the bed next to her and brings her fingertips to his mouth for a kiss, his eyes blazing again. "People damn well *better* look at you differently, scarecrow, but not because you're broken. Because you're a fucking phoenix, and if anyone ever tries to tell you otherwise, you tell them there are two hundred and six bones in the human body, and your man Jude will *gladly* be carving theirs into two hundred and six works of art, just so you can have the pleasure of displaying them on your nightstand."

West cracks up. "Okay, so how many bones does a gargoyle have? Because if *Draegan* starts treating me like I'm made of glass, I want to be sure to get the threat right."

"Draegan wouldn't do that," Jude says firmly, shaking his head. "For all his huffing and puffing, he couldn't possibly see you as anything but what you truly are."

"Hmm. And what's that?" she teases.

"A very beautiful, very brave, *very* sexy goddess. One with a great arse, the most perfect little mouth, and a whole bunch of other attributes I'll be dreaming about the rest of my eternal life."

"Cosigned," I say. "And Jude? If you're going to slide into my spot as the flirty one of the operation, does that mean I can be the psycho? And finally play with your bone saw?"

"No need to limit ourselves with labels, Augustine. I can be flirty *and* psychotic, as can you. But touch my bone saw, and you'll find out just how quickly I can flip the switch."

I laugh. "Don't scare the witchling, psycho."

"I can handle it," she says. "Seriously. I'm good with anything, as long as you don't treat me like I'm damaged goods."

"Are you kidding me?" I snort. "If you *really* want to talk about damaged goods, may I present exhibit A?" I gesture toward Jude's face. "I've been staring at *that* for longer than I care to remember. Downright horrifying."

"If only his mother felt the same way," Jude mock-whispers behind a clawed hand. "He'll never admit it, but there's a chance I'm his father."

"That would make things *really* awkward in the bedroom," I say, "so maybe it's best if you don't join us next time, Jude."

"Don't even think about it!" West laughs, but it quickly trails off into a yawn.

I exchange another glance with Jude, who nods in silent agreement.

Our girl needs to rest.

And her gargoyles have some plotting to do.

Jude presses a kiss to her forehead, his eyes shining with a tenderness I've never seen before. "You don't have to hide any part of yourself from us, scarecrow. You've got nothing to be ashamed of—remember that."

"Jude's right," I say softly. "You're beautiful. Every inch of you, inside and out. No one can ever take that from you."

"And if they bloody try," Jude says, "they're going to find out what it's like to live with their internal organs on the outside."

West wrinkles her nose, adorable as ever. "That... doesn't sound very fun."

"Well, not for *them*," Jude says. "But for me? It's a regular riot, darling. Trust me."

"I'll take your word." Her soft laughter threatens to undo me.

Being inside her tonight, sharing her with Jude, being so close to her... It was indescribable.

But it's the laugh that does me in. Every fucking time.

The fact that anyone tried to take that from her... It's beyond comprehension.

And it can't go unpunished. It just can't.

"Who were the others?" I ask suddenly, the calmness in

my voice belying the jackhammering of my heart. "The boys who showed up in the tunnel."

"I... I'm not sure I remember them all."

"The names of those who've hurt us stay with us, scarecrow," Jude says, and the raw emotion in his voice—another first—makes my chest hurt. "Even when they've long forgotten ours. That's why the memories keep haunting us."

"Do the dark fae still haunt you?" she whispers. "The ones who cursed you?"

"They do," he says, and I nod.

Not a night goes by when I don't think about the fae king. The soldiers. I'm sure it's the same for Jude, Drae, and Rook. Just like I'm sure West knows the name of every one of her tormentors, even if she doesn't want to speak them all out loud.

She sighs. "It was a long time ago."

Jude frowns, tracing his thumb along her cheek. "No. It wasn't."

"I know why you're asking," she says, "and as much as I love your 'burn down the world for your girl' energy, you don't have to fight my battles. Especially my old ones."

"Yes we do," Jude and I say at the same time.

She looks up at me again, her eyes like two bright jewels sparkling in the darkness. "Why are you guys being so adamant about this?"

"Because you're *ours*, Westlyn Avery," I say fiercely. "And we protect what's ours."

"Draegan said something like that to me my first night here," she says. "Back then it felt like a threat."

"And now?" I ask.

"Now..." She trails off into a contented sigh and rolls onto her hip away from me, tucking her hands under the pillow and settling in for a good day's rest. "Now it just feels like home."

"Because it is," I whisper, lifting the damp hair off the back of her neck and pressing a kiss there, just at the base of her hairline. West lets out a murmur of pleasure, but a white-hot spark sizzles painfully across my lips, and that cold, otherworldly darkness sweeps right through me again.

Stomach roiling, I pull back and take a look at her neck, but there's nothing there but her smooth, unmarked skin.

"The sun will be up soon," West says, her voice heavy with a mix of exhaustion and disappointment. "I hate that you guys have to go. I wish I could turn to stone, too."

"No, my beautiful witchling," I whisper, tucking her hair back into place and getting to my feet. "You don't."

"Get some sleep," Jude says. "We'll all be down in the kitchen eating Auggie's night-breakfast before you know it, and no, that's not a euphemism. Though I'm pretty sure the three of us could turn it into one."

"And now we've got *that* to look forward to." I force a laugh, then turn off the lamp on the nightstand. "Sweet dreams, West."

Now it feels like home...

Her words are still echoing through my mind as Jude and I step out into the hallway. The moment the bedroom door clicks shut behind us, that cold wind races through my bones again, gripping my heart and doubling me over.

"What is it?" Jude asks, his hand on my shoulder. "You've got that heebie-jeebie look again."

I nod. "Started when I kissed the back of her neck. I felt something—some kind of spark. Hurt like a bitch."

"Static?"

"No, Jude. Not static."

"Fuck."

"No shit." I suck in a few deep breaths and wait for the nausea to pass, then finally stand up straight again. "There's something we're missing here. Something about her past— about her origins. I can feel it."

"You still think we're dealing with some sort of unformed fae entity?"

"That's what my gut says. I just don't know whether it's attached to her, or..."

"Or what?"

"Or part of her."

Jude closes his eyes, cursing under his breath. When he looks at me again, his eyes blaze with determination, his jaw set. "One thing at a time, mate. Right now—"

"Yeah, I know. I'm with you." I nod, knowing exactly where his head is at. "You get those names?"

"Jacob Pomeroy, Alonzo Florentine, and some tosser

called Full Metal Jacket. Name like that, I'm sure he's left a trail of achievements."

"Should make him easy to track."

"Assuming they're all shadow magic society pricks, they're likely still in the city. Won't be hard for Rook to find out where they live and work. Then I can make my move."

"*We* can make *our* move. We're in this together, brother."

"You know it's gonna get ugly, right?"

"Burning down the world for our girl? Worth it."

"No, Augs. We're not going to burn down the world. We're just going to burn *them*."

I follow him down the stairs and into the study for one last drink before bed. Pouring us both a glass of whiskey, I say, "Honestly, I kind of prefer the organs-on-the-outside idea."

He takes his drink and glares at me. "You're still not touching the bone saw."

"Fair enough. Just promise me one thing."

"Name it."

"Those fuckers do *not* get out of this alive."

He flashes his most terrifying, completely unhinged grin, his eyes alight with the promise of violence. "Not only will they not get out of this alive, but we'll be making their final moments so *bloody* excruciating they'll leave a trail of tears and piss all the way to hell."

I lift my glass and nod. "Cheers to that, brother. Cheers to that."

CHAPTER SIX

WESTLYN

Your little games are merely delaying the inevitable. You belong to me, witch...

I awaken with a strangled gasp, my naked body slick with sweat, my heart thundering as if I've been running marathons in my sleep.

You belong to me, witch...

The cruel voice bounces around my skull, and I swear I still feel a presence around me, touching me, *smothering* me like some kind of sleep paralysis demon.

Only this one's worse, because I'm pretty sure it wasn't some random, no-name demon stalking my dreams.

It was Zorakkov.

Rubbing the chill and the last vestiges of his touch from my arms, I sit up in Auggie's bed, the room slowly coming into focus.

Outside, the moon shines bright—I slept longer than I

meant to. Lucinda and Huxley are perched on the windowsill, quietly keeping watch.

"Good morning, my loves. Or rather, good evening." I give them each a few strokes between their wings. "Were you two here the whole time I slept?"

Huxley shivers with pleasure, and Lucinda playfully nips my thumb.

"Thank you. I appreciate the company."

Feeling a bit better, I stretch and get out of bed, wrapping myself up in a sheet and checking out the bedroom. I didn't pay much attention to the decor when Auggie first carried me in here after our library adventures last night, and between the threesome and intense conversation that followed, the walls were no more than photo-covered background noise.

But now, I check out the pictures in earnest.

They're everywhere—framed black and white shots in a variety of sizes from wallets to posters, mostly hung on the walls, some displayed on the dressers. Every single image was shot at night, all featuring the same subject matter.

Gargoyles.

There are only a few of the guys themselves—one of Rook bent over a book in the library, his brow creased in concentration. Draegan pouring a drink at the bar in the study, glaring at the camera as if he's one second from smashing it. Jude showing off a carved white rose that was probably made out of a femur.

But most of his collection showcases the stone variety

of gargoyle. I recognize a lot of the buildings as famous locations from around the city, while others are completely new to me. There are several from the Blackmoor Cathedral as well—the same ones I wished upon the night of my wedding.

"Don't keep me in suspense, witchling," Auggie's deep voice rumbles from behind me, and I turn toward him, a smile stretching across my face. "What do you think of my work?"

"You shot all of these yourself?"

"Guilty."

"They're amazing! Seriously, Auggie. They should be in a magazine."

"Some of them are."

"Really?"

He nods. "Not the ones of the guys, of course. But the architectural ones. Every few decades, the human obsession with gargoyles and grotesques kicks up again, and there's a call for them in architectural and travel magazines. I try to submit them when I can."

"Do they pay you?"

"Yes—I put it all back into our restoration projects. The way I see it, these guys deserve it more than I do. I'm just the guy behind the camera, but they're..." He trails off, a hint of sadness in his eyes as he reaches past me to straighten one of the frames—a shot of a gargoyle with his wings outstretched, perched on the cornice of a building as if he's about to leap off and swoop down on the unsuspecting pedestrians below. "Anyway, it's a good opportunity for me to share my love of photography with humans without actually having to talk to any of them."

"Are all these gargoyles entrusted to your care?"

"Every single one."

I scan the room, trying to get a sense of how many there are. Hundreds. Thousands, maybe. I don't even know if he's photographed all of them.

But then I notice something else.

"They're all male," I say. "Unless this is one of those things where the females look identical to the males. Like dwarves?"

He smiles, but it's not a happy one—his dimple barely makes an appearance. His eyes mist, and then he lowers them, shaking his head. "There aren't any female gargoyles," he says softly. "Not real ones, anyway. There never were."

"What? But—"

"So." He looks up at me and takes my hands, his smile firmly back in place. Still no dimple, but it's clear whatever's going on in his head, he doesn't want to share it. "How are you feeling? Did you sleep okay?"

I want to ask him again about the females, but I suspect it's related to their curse, and he made it clear last night he's not ready to talk about that just yet.

Returning his smile, I say, "I slept like a *rock*. Just like you guys. Get it? Rock?"

"Oh, you're a little comedian now, is that it?" His dimple finally flashes, the sight of it lighting me up inside.

"*I* am downright hilarious." I stretch up on my toes and try to loop my arms around his neck, but he's too damn big.

"Need a little help, witchling?" Sliding his hands under my ass, Auggie hauls me up, pulling me close. The sheet bunches up around my waist, exposing my bare pussy.

"Oh, yeah," he says. "That's *definitely* better."

"For you or for me?"

"You tell me." He draws me closer and I wrap my legs around his hips, his cock teasing me from just beneath his loincloth. He's hard for me again, and I can't help the moan that escapes my lips at the feel of him.

"Evening stone," I say. "Gargoyle equivalent of morning wood."

He cracks up at that, and I'm laughing right along with him, the mood suddenly brighter than it's been since he first carried me in here last night.

"What time is it, anyway?" I ask. "I feel like I slept for a week."

"A bit after seven. We almost woke you earlier, but decided you needed your sleep." Nodding at my corvid companions on the windowsill, he says, "We only let the ravens in because they were pacing outside the door for an hour and Draegan was worried about the finish on his hardwoods."

"When is he *not* worried about his damned hardwoods?" I laugh again, threading my fingers into the back of his silky hair. "Where is everyone else, anyway? Off to the city tonight?"

"Draegan's on a call with some building inspector or another. Jude's with Rook in the library, following up on a few leads. Apparently, Rook's cameras caught someone coming and going from Hunter's apartment four times in the last two days—a woman dressed in scrubs, carrying out bags of medical waste. They're waiting for word from our contact at the DMV about the plates on her car, and he's running her photo through some facial recognition program to see if it matches anyone from the wedding."

"It wasn't Hunter's mother?"

"No—I saw the video. Definitely not Celine Forsythe. Not Eloise, either."

"Do you think he's having more procedures done?"

"That's the thought, but we're still not sure why. The whole thing is a mystery." He sighs, then slides a hand down to cup my ass. Through a mischievous grin, he says, "Still sore?"

"A little, yeah. But it's the good kind of sore, you know?"

"Oh, I know." He winks, his eyes darkening with lust. In a low rumble that has my thighs clenching, he says, "Do you trust me, witchling?"

After last night, how could I not? He and Jude took care of me. Not just in bed, but through the dark confessions that followed—through all the things I'd been too terrified to admit until my gargoyles held me in their strong arms and made me feel safe and seen.

"Absolutely," I say without hesitation.

"Glad to hear it." Another slow smile stretches across

his lips, and then he's carrying me back to the bed, drop-ping me in the center. "Now turn around, get on your knees, and grab the headboard. Oh, and Westlyn? Lose the sheet."

The commanding tone in his voice leaves no room for argument. Even the ravens sense the trouble brewing—they leap from the sill and zoom right out the door.

Sparing him one last grin of my own, I do as he asks, my pussy already throbbing with anticipation, all of last night's aches a distant memory compared to the intense pleasure I know is coming next.

He kicks the door shut as I get into position, then he strips and climbs into bed behind me, the mattress dipping under his weight.

"So lovely," he whispers, the tips of his claws tracing delicate circles on my bare ass. "So perfect."

Wet and ready for him, I arch my back and wait for the press of his demanding cock, but it never comes.

Instead, he wraps his hands around my thighs, urging me wider and lowering his mouth to my flesh. He leaves a trail of hot, soft kisses along the curve where my left thigh meets my ass, then moves to the other side, his breath a hot, merciless tease across my pussy.

Back and forth he works his slow, seductive magic, driving me right to the edge but never over it, making my thighs quake with need.

"You... you are *very* mean," I pant.

"No, witchling. I'm the nice one, remember?" He lets out a dark chuckle. Then, as if to prove his point, he finally

—*finally!*—presses his lips to my aching center and unfurls his tongue, giving me a long, languid lick.

I gasp as a shiver of ecstasy rolls down my spine, and then he's...

Oh, *goddess.* He's *everywhere.*

His tongue is so long, so thick, he leaves no part of me wanting, the tip drawing maddening circles around my clit while the rest undulates against my entrance, his deep moans vibrating right through me.

Tightening his grip on my thighs, he spears my pussy with that perfect tongue, then draws back, licking and teasing his way to the very spot where Jude so ruthlessly claimed me last night.

A hot, delicate swirl around the rim, and then...

Holy fuck... Is he seriously going to—

"Augustine!" I gasp as his tongue delves inside, fresh waves of pleasure rolling and cresting through my entire body, each one driving me closer and closer to bliss, his big hands gripping my ass and spreading me wider as my gargoyle explores me with soft, hot strokes.

I'm totally open for him, totally exposed. Maybe I should be embarrassed or shy or *completely* freaking out that this is actually happening, but I can't. It feels too fucking good. There's no room for anything but euphoria as he licks and sucks and moans and works his magic, one seductively sinful kiss at a time.

Every moment with him unlocks another first for me,

yet somehow, it feels as if we've been doing this together my entire life.

I close my eyes and arch my back again, grinding back against his relentless tongue-lashing. Pinpricks of light begin to dance behind my eyelids. The first tingles of the impending explosion ripple through me, and Auggie rolls onto his back, gripping my ass and hauling me against his mouth, his tail sliding around to tease my tight hole while his lips move to my clit, sucking and nibbling, hot breath ghosting across my slick pussy as he groans inside me, and then…

"Right there," I whisper. "Goddess, yes. Right there!"

The orgasm detonates, shock waves of pleasure sizzling through every part of me as Auggie continues to devour me, his claws scraping against my thighs, his tail and tongue tag-teaming my most sensitive spots, again and again and again until I can no longer hold the headboard, no longer even hold myself up.

Auggie lifts me and flips us over so he's on top, his mouth shining, his eyes half-lidded. "From now on, I want my first meal of every night to be you."

I laugh. "You drive a hard bargain, Mr. Lamont, but I think we can come to an agreement."

I reach for him, eager to feel his hard cock in my hands, in my mouth, in all the places he just licked.

But before I get close, he grabs my wrist and kisses my palm. "Later, witchling. When you've fully recovered from last night."

"Keep doing what you're doing to me, and I'll *never* recover."

"Hmm. We'll see." He presses a soft, wet kiss to my mouth, then says, "Let's say we head downstairs and fix you up some of Auggie's patented night-breakfast."

"Again, you drive a hard bargain, but sure. If you *insist* on feeding me, I guess I shouldn't disappoint you."

"Excellent. Any requests?" He rises from the bed and holds out a hand, helping me to my feet. "Your breakfast wish is my command."

"How about baked oatmeal, fruit salad, an almond joy latte, and maybe another thorough tonguing?"

"Done, done, done, and *done*," he says with a grin, and that pretty much settles it:

I'm *never* leaving this magical place.

CHAPTER SEVEN

ROOK

Long before the internet invaded our lives, long before computers, long before the printing press allowed for widespread distribution of volumes upon volumes of accumulated knowledge—hell, even before I became a gargoyle—I always prided myself on my capacity for logic and reason. On my ability to keep a clear head, to work through complex issues one methodical step at a time. Rational thought is, after all, the foundation of a functional society— a place where things make sense, where every action has a predictable reaction, where even the most challenging problems have viable solutions.

But tonight, as Jude sits across from me at one of the library tables and recounts the horrifying tale of abuse West endured as a child, I lose the ability to think straight. Every one of his words fries another circuit in my brain, throwing my ordered thoughts into chaos. It's all I can do to stay focused on his voice, on the gruesome details of her experience, on the names of the monsters who committed such an atrocious crime.

Jude's not faring much better.

To an outside observer, sure, Jude would probably appear calm and rational. No smashing furniture, no vicious outbursts, not even the twitch of an eyelid or the ripple of a dark wing to give him away.

But I know him too well to believe he's truly taking this in stride. The fact that he's holding back right now? Nothing but a warning of the carnage to come.

And this time, I won't be attempting to win him over with sound arguments against violence or a point-by-point list of all the reasons we need to lie low. I won't insist that he let the magical community handle their own. I won't remind him that the so-named men of shadow and stone are already under suspicion for murder and extortion and the alleged kidnapping of a young bride, and we can't afford to draw additional attention to ourselves.

No. This time, when Jude pours the gasoline? I'll be the one handing him the fucking flamethrower.

After what feels like another fifteen hundred years of pure torture, he finally gets to the end of it.

I close my eyes, trying to breathe through it. It's like living fire, this feeling inside my chest. Eating through my veins. Incinerating my bones.

"Rook." The firm command of his voice and the touch

of a warm hand over mine brings me back to the moment, and I open my eyes, meeting Jude's across the table.

Once again, I'm struck by the stone-cold calm in his outward appearance.

"I need you on this, brother. Focus."

I take a deep breath and nod, picturing our sweet little witch sitting in the very spot he now occupies, sipping her latte, feet swishing under the table as she flips through another lore book helping me search for clues about her past. About ours.

For her, I remind myself. For her, I can pull it together.

"Names," I say, booting up my laptop and pulling up the voter registration, organ donor, and criminal records databases for New York State. I haven't been able to hack into the DMV on my own yet, but if I can't track the fuckers myself, I'll send the names to our contact there. She just sent over the details on Hunter's healthcare visitor, but she's always happy for more work.

If one thing's been constant since the establishment of this sprawling metropolis, it's this:

It's a rare city employee who *isn't* thrilled to take our money in exchange for a little insider info.

Jude rattles off two names—Jacob Pomeroy and Alonzo Florentine. Starting with Pomeroy, I enter all possible spellings into the databases and two different online public records aggregators, then submit my queries.

Because this? This is a thing I can do. An actual task,

logical and reasonable. It settles me, grounds me, keeps me sane when all I want to do is fucking explode.

"That's it?" I ask. "Just the two guys?"

"And another cocksucker called Full Metal Jacket. Westlyn never knew his real name."

"Same age as the others?"

"Yeah, they were all school chums. A bunch of other arseholes showed up too, but she claims she doesn't remember them. We'll give her some time and see if she changes her mind."

"Social media," I say. "That's our in."

While the databases are looking for matches, I grab my tablet and pull up all the apps, double-checking I've got my security settings on lockdown. Anonymous is the *only* way to go here. The last thing we need is these bastards figuring out they're being tracked, or worse—turning the tables on us and coming after West for a reunion tour.

"Talk me through it, resident genius," Jude says, coming around to my side of the table to watch over my shoulder. "My app-sleuthing skills are as rusty as a metal arsehole, balls-deep in the river."

"Hate to break it to you, Jude, but..." I laugh, grateful for a momentary reprieve from the fire raging inside me. "Your similes could use some finessing, too."

"You get what I'm saying though, yeah?"

"What you're saying defies all logic and paints a horrifying picture, but... Yes, it's clear you need some pointers on using the internet to track down our enemies."

"Brilliant. Let's have it, then."

"Well, we've got the names of two out of the three ring-leaders, and the third is possibly still using the same alias. So that's where we start. We analyze the social footprint from dickheads one and two, along with any socials with a New York IP address using the Full Metal Jacket handle or some variation thereof. If we don't get any hits in New York, I'll expand the search, starting with the locations of common VPN servers they might be using to obscure their locations. From there, we can cross-reference the friend and follower lists and narrow down the rest of the friend group. Since they openly talked about magic and summoning demons, it's likely they're all mages, and mages in this city are a tight group. I'd be surprised if they're not still in close contact."

Jude fists my hair, giving my head a playful shake. "Ah, Rook. I've got no idea what in the *bleeding* hell you're talking about, but times like this, I wanna just grab you by the hair and kiss you. *With* tongue."

"I *really* hope you're still speaking in metaphor."

"We've already established I'm not smart enough for metaphors." Laughing, he finally releases me and heads to the kitchen. "Beer?"

"No thanks, but I'll take a kombucha if there's any left."

He returns with two bottles—beer for himself, an orange-mango kombucha for me. "Fresh out of bee pollen, I'm afraid."

"I'll survive." I crack open the bottle, then peek at my

laptop. We've already got a few hits on Pomeroy, complete with photos, recent addresses going back five years, and a list of known associates and family members.

The asshole has a rap sheet a mile long too, but all the charges were mysteriously dropped.

Every fucking time.

No matter. He's definitely our guy. He looks about the same age as West, but that's not what confirms it for me.

It's the family members.

"Oh, shit." I set down the kombucha and tab over to my encrypted email, where the details on Hunter's healthcare visitor are still sitting in my inbox. "It's his mother, Jude. Belinda Eckhardt is Jacob Pomeroy's mother."

"Who the fuck is Belinda Eckhardt?"

Ignoring him, I export all the details on Pomeroy into a new document, send it to the printer, then submit similar queries for Alonzo Florentine. While that's running, I pull up one of my own databases—the list of Forsythe wedding guests we've been able to positively identify so far.

Bingo. Belinda Eckhardt is on the list. No wonder her name sounded familiar.

No Pomeroy yet, but hey. I'm just getting warmed up.

I import his photos from the report and run them against our footage from the cathedral cameras. It takes less than five seconds for my program to confirm the match, serving up a shot of him in the third pew from the altar, sitting right next to his mother.

"This has shadow magic society written all over it," I say, tabbing back to the query results on Florentine. His rap sheet isn't quite as extensive as Pomeroy's, but for the most part, their lives seem to be running on parallel tracks.

Once a fucking moron, always a fucking moron.

I print out those results too. I don't recognize any of the names on Florentine's list of associates, but when I export his photos into my wedding database, we get another immediate match.

Bastard's sitting right there on the other side of Pomeroy. The rest of the people in their row are women, but it's not a stretch to assume Full Metal Jacket was at the wedding, too.

And if he was, I'll find him.

"Far be it from me to interrupt a genius on the verge of discovery," Jude says, "but any time you feel like clueing me in, I'm here for it. Preferably before that vein on your forehead bursts."

"Huh?" I glance up at him, my mind still churning through this new info, connecting dots and opening up all new lines of questioning and—

"You've got this vein, see?" Jude taps a spot above his eyebrow. "Throbbing like a cock in—"

"Hold that simile. *Please.*" I head over to the printer to

collect the pages on our shadow mage pricks. Flipping through them, I give Jude the rundown on my findings.

"So this Belinda Eckhardt," he says. "She's shadow magic society as well?"

"Yes. Also a doctor working at—drumroll, please—Garrison Medical."

"All roads lead back to that fucking hospital, don't they? Maybe I should blow it up."

"Focus, Jude. Focus."

"Right. Shadow magic society... You were saying?"

"So far, all the guests we've been able to identify—including now Pomeroy and Florentine—are connected to that organization. There are only about thirty or so more guests we haven't confirmed names on, but I'd bet this entire library they're all *Forsythe* guests."

"Westlyn certainly didn't invite anyone. And her father had no friends left to invite. According to West, he alienated everyone in their circle."

"Right. And Eloise? You can't convince me *she* married for love. At this point, I'm counting her as a Forsythe guest, too."

"Which means everyone at that wedding is either part of or deeply connected to the shadow magic society. Even the high priest."

"Explains why no one tried to help her when things took a turn for the worse during the ceremony." The realization sets my blood to boiling again. "They were all fucking in on it."

"Starting long before the wedding."

"Right. So now we've got the Forsythes, including their son Hunter, who seems to be a vessel for Zorakkov. We've got three men who terrorized West as a teenager, which was a decade ago. And more than a decade before *that*, we've got Hunter getting some kind of mysterious medical treatments at the same hospital where West was born and her evil stepmother worked in pediatrics."

"And those treatments started the day after our girl was born."

"Now there's another doctor from their circle—also a Garrison Hospital employee—visiting his apartment, and we haven't seen him leaving at all since the wedding."

"So where do we start, Rook? The way I see it, they're all going down. Question is, who goes first?"

I toss the stacks of papers on the table in front of him and reclaim my seat on the bench. "There's everything you need to track down Pomeroy and Florentine. I'll let you know when I finish with the socials—shouldn't take me too long to find this Full Metal Jacket douchebag."

Jude looks over the paperwork and nods. "And Pomeroy's bitch of a mother?"

"Same address."

"Oh, I love it when you make my job easier." He grins, the wheels turning behind his eyes. "Nothing like a two-fer to give an event that extra special something."

"How is this all playing out, then? You planning to take care of it offsite?"

Jude likes to work from home, but when there's more than one perp involved, that complicates things.

"Auggie and I still need to nail down the final plan, but the way I see it... Yeah. I'm thinking the old Ryker Meat Packing Plant for this one—that'll work out nicely. So, we pop on down to Hell's Kitchen and grab Pomeroy and his mum, then zip down to Chelsea for Alonzo. The plant's just a stone's throw from there. Once you track Full Metal *Jackoff*, we'll figure out where he is on our route and plan accordingly."

"You flying?"

"Nah, too complicated with all those bodies. We'll take Draegan's Escalade."

I laugh. "Oh, he'll love that. Better not get any blood on the seats."

"Wouldn't dream of it."

Swirling my untouched bottle of kombucha, I say, "You sure it's not too complicated with the mother involved? Maybe you should bring her in separately."

"What's a complication but an opportunity in disguise?" He glances up from the paperwork, his grin manic. "Since their brutalization of our little scarecrow was a family affair, their... *interrogations* will be, too."

"You're going to eliminate them, I presume?" *Hope*. I don't say that word out loud, but I know he can read it in my eyes.

"Not right away, no."

Again, the rational part of my mind kicks in, begging me

to talk him out of this. Three men and one of their mothers, all members of the shadow magic society, all with extremely powerful allies, all connected to the botched wedding and the Archmage's gruesome plans for West... We're in dangerous territory here. Far more than we've ever faced since the fae cursed us to this life.

But now, when I hold his determined gaze across the table, all that rational thought evaporates.

Once more I think of West, hanging out with me here in the library, asking me a hundred and one questions about fae and demon lore, her inquisitive eyes bright. I think of her laughter, and her raven companions, and the way she feels like she's always been part of us, and the way my heart skips whenever she walks into the room.

And then, in a voice so dark I barely recognize it, I say, "I want you to make them fucking *bleed*."

Jude nods. "You know I will, brother."

"I don't care what happens to the boys, but we need the woman alive. She's our best shot at getting intel on those medical treatments and what the connection is to West's birth."

"Shall I gift wrap her for you, or just chain her up naked in the basement?"

"I'll leave the presentation to you." I take off my glasses and rub my eyes, a wave of exhaustion rolling over me despite the fact that I've only been up for a couple of hours. "Jude? How is West?"

"As lovely as always. Why?"

"I mean... How is she handling all of this? I know you guys are... close."

"She's strong, Rook. Blows me away with it, tell you the truth. I know the four of us have been *through* it, but..." Jude lets out a heavy sigh. "She's been on her own her entire life. Us? We've got each other, for better or worse. But this girl... no one has *ever* had her back. Not her parents, not her teachers, not her so-called fiancé. When I think about how scared she must've been... Human girl, twelve fucking years old..." A shudder ripples through him, head to toe. When he meets my eyes again, his own are glassy with unshed tears. "There's something else. Auggie... He's still getting those bad vibes."

He tells me about what happened last night—what Auggie said about kissing her and his thoughts about the fae entity.

"Have you told her?" I ask.

He shakes his head. "She was asleep when we talked about it. Auggie thinks we should wait until we know for sure what we're dealing with."

"I see his point, but we promised her no secrets, remember?" I finally take a sip of the kombucha, then say, "I can bring it up to her later if you're okay with that. We've got a date with the Codex—perfect segue to talking about freaky fae phenomena."

He paces the room, considering, then finally nods.

"Yeah, all right. Auggie and I need to focus on these mages, anyway."

"Agreed."

"Besides," he says, "Westlyn trusts you. Says you're—and I quote—basically the sweetest guy *ever*."

I can't help the smile that spreads across my face. Likely a pretty good blush, too.

Jude rolls his eyes. "And on *that* vomit-inducing note, I'm off. Thanks again for the lowdown on our boys."

"You making your move tonight?"

"Nah, Augs and I still need time to strategize. Plus, it'd be better to roll out when Draegan's not home, especially if we've got any chance of borrowing his Escalade unnoticed."

"Good point. But I wouldn't keep the plans secret from him entirely. You know how he gets."

"Auggie's already telling him about the *overall* plan. Just not that minor, insignificant bit about the Escalade."

"Good. Timing?"

"We'll shoot for tomorrow night. Right now, I need to find our girl. Tell her where we're at with all this."

"You sure that's prudent?"

"Not at all. But like you said... No secrets, right?" He tries for a flippant grin, but it quickly pulls into a frown, his eyes turning serious. Giving my wing an affectionate squeeze, he says softly, "We're all in this together, Rook. And from here on out, 'all of us' includes Westlyn Avery."

I nod my agreement and wish him luck, but not because I'm worried about how West will handle the news.

I wish him luck because for the first time in our impossibly long, impossibly tangled immortal lives together, I'm pretty sure Jude Hendrix—the violent, crazy, fiercely loyal gargoyle who carves up the bones of his enemies and gets off on the scent of freshly spilled blood—is falling in love.

CHAPTER NINE

JUDE

"No peeking, darling. We don't want to ruin the surprise, do we?"

"I'm so not peeking!" Westlyn laughs, anxiously strumming her fingers on the breakfast table, her eyes half-squinted, the little cheater.

Silently, I sit on the bench beside her, then lean in close and whisper, "I should make you wait another hour just to punish you for your underhanded tactics."

She yelps and turns toward me, and before she even opens her eyes, I haul her into my lap and bite her earlobe.

"All right, fine," I say. "Since it's become *painfully* obvious I can't trust you to follow instructions, go ahead and look."

She opens her eyes, and the sweetest little gasp rushes out from her lips. "Jude! What the... Are these... um... are these Randall's—"

"Kneecaps," I say brightly, and she picks one up for closer inspection. "Rather, they *were* his kneecaps, and now they're tiny bowls for tiny crackers—just the right size for your birds. Completely sanitized, not to worry. Rook built me a machine that does it. Kind of like a high-powered dishwasher. Gets off all the sticky bits."

She's silent for a moment, tracing her thumb over their polished curves.

I'm about to tell her it's all a joke, because I'm pretty damn sure I just found her hard limit, but then, almost reverently, she says, "You etched all these flowers on the outside by hand?"

"Well, yeah. Way I see it, birds and flowers go together, right?"

She turns and tilts her head back to meet my eyes, her own shining with emotion. "You made these for me?"

"Don't sound so shocked, scarecrow. Isn't that what a boyfriend does? Makes presents for his girlfriend?"

Her eyes brighten, a smile flickering at the corners of her mouth. "Is that what we are?" she teases. "Boyfriend and girlfriend?"

"Honestly, I'd prefer the term *man*-friend, or even beast-friend—more appropriate, don't you think? But boyfriend is more in keeping with the current vernacular."

"No, I like beastfriend *way* better. But to answer your question, I'm not sure about the presents. I've never had a boy-man-beastfriend before."

"Well, you do now, darling. And *this* beastfriend? He's

gonna spoil you rotten." I tighten my hold around her waist and sniff the side of her neck, breathing in her fresh, clean scent. "You *and* your birds."

She laughs. "Really?"

"The three of you—sorry, four. There's one more, right? Jean-Pierre?—you're a package deal. A bit weird, if you ask me, but hey. No kink-shaming in *this* house."

She huffs with faux indignation. "Once again, ladies and gents, the guy who carves bowls out of kneecaps is calling *me* weird."

"Oh, I meant it as a compliment."

With another grin, she says, "Now I know your secret, Jude Hendrix."

"That so? Let's hear it, then."

"You've got a big... heart." She presses her hand flat against my chest. "Huge. *Massive*."

"A big, massive *heart*? *That's* what you're on about?" I gather her closer, threading my claws into her hair and brushing a kiss to the corner of her mouth. "Does this mean you like your gift? I made some dice for Rook, so if you're not into the bowls, we could ask him for a trade."

"Dice?"

"From the..." I grin and tap my teeth. "Not Randall's, though. Smashed his to smithereens with a hammer— nothing to be salvaged there."

"Sorry, I'm still trying to wrap my head around the fact that you made dice out of someone's teeth."

"Oh, sure. Bit small for real gaming, but Rook likes

collecting things like that. Little game pieces and dice and figurines. It's all child's play, if you ask me, but I sure did enjoy drilling all the holes and filling them with resin. Precision work, that. Requires a real fine touch. Fortunately, as you know..." I flip her around so she's straddling me, and slide my hands up under her shorts, claws brushing along the curves of her arse. "A fine touch is another of my *many* talents."

"Accurate," she breathes. Then, with another laugh, "You know, I'd hate to deprive Rook of such a cool gift. I'm good with the bowls."

"You sure?"

"They're perfect. Huxley and Lucinda are out in the orchard now, but I know they'll go bat-shit crazy for them. Well, *bird*-shit crazy. I can't wait for them to try them out."

"Seems I'm pretty good at this beastfriend stuff."

"You are," she concedes. "But what about Auggie?"

"I'm working on a gravy terrine for him, but I need a bit more time attaching the handle to the skull—"

"No, I mean... Can he be my beastfriend too?"

"I don't know, scarecrow," I tease, knowing damn well I'd *never* say no to something that puts such a smile on her pretty face. "What's *that* gargoyle bringing to the table? Not my priceless works of art, that's for sure."

"He feeds me. Like, constantly. All my favorites. And lots of stuff I've never even tried before, too."

"Anyone could feed you, darling."

"Yeah, but not everyone keeps a running list of all my allergies and dietary restrictions, and goes out of their way to find substitute ingredients, and—"

"Oh, for fuck's sake, you've made your point. Auggie's in." I laugh. "Anyone else on this beastfriend wish list of yours?"

"Hmm. *Maybe*."

"Great." I brush a trail of kisses along her jawline, slowly working my way to her ear. "Clearly, I'm going to have to up my game to compete with Rook."

She sighs softly, sliding her hands up to curl around my horns, giving them a gentle stroke. Then, in a sweet little whisper, "You're doing just fine, Jude."

Fuck, the way she says my name, the way her lips round out in the middle of it... Drives me wild every fucking time.

Holding her like this, feeling the solid weight and warmth of her in my arms while she touches me, while she whispers my name like that...

The thought that anyone ever hurt her before... That we weren't around to protect her back then...

The rage I've worked so hard to keep in check since last night threatens to erupt.

"Westlyn," I say softly, my voice trembling.

"Hmm, busting out the real name?" She draws back, cradles my face between her hands. "You must be more freaked out than I thought."

"I'm not freaked out. Just..." *Fuck*, I don't have the

words for this. Rook's the one with all the smart things to say, all the right similes and whatnot. Me? I can bust heads and slice off appendages any night of the week, but when it comes to getting my jumbled-up thoughts across, I'm fucking useless.

"That's partly why I didn't want to tell you guys," she says, tracing her thumbs across my cheeks. "It's... it's a lot to process, and maybe I shouldn't have laid it on you. Besides, it's all in the past now, and—"

"Hey. *Hey.*" I close my eyes and touch my forehead to hers, wishing I could *literally* just fucking breathe her in, keep her locked inside me where no one could ever touch her. But that's not possible, and I'd fucking miss holding her like this, and hearing her say my name, and watching her feed her birds and push Drae's buttons and moan over Auggie's cooking and fuck... all the hundreds of little ways she's invaded my heart. So all I can do is the next best thing —take care of her. Fucking take *care* of her.

"Your past is part of your life, scarecrow," I say softly. "And now you're part of *our* lives. I bloody *hate* that it happened to you, but I'm glad you told us. I want to know about you. All the big and little and beautiful and terrible things that shaped you into *this* woman, right here. Because *this* woman?" I sigh against her lips. "She's pretty damn perfect."

She doesn't say anything. Just tilts her head and kisses me, soft and slow and delicious.

When we break for air, I slide my claws out of her

shorts and take her hands, pressing a kiss to each of her fingers. To the ring on her thumb—the one I gave her the first night she came to Blackmoor.

"No one will *ever* hurt you like that again, Westlyn Avery," I say. "*That* is a promise. And as for the ones who've already done it, they're not long for this world."

"Jude." She closes her eyes and shakes her head. "I'm not even sure if they're still in the city. They could be in Topeka for all we—"

"Chelsea, actually. And Hell's Kitchen." I tell her about Rook's databases, all the details he learned about the soon-to-be dead mages who hurt her, along with the mystery doctor visiting Hunter—Pomeroy's mother.

"Wow," she says. "Rook works fast."

"He's our spymaster, scarecrow. And he's very, very good at his job."

She opens her eyes and threads her fingers behind my neck. "How many times do I have to tell you? You don't have to go on some bloody rampage to avenge my honor."

"I don't *have* to, no." I grin, trying to force a bit more levity into my voice. Trying to keep that fury at bay. "I'm doing it for the pure pleasure of it. You know how I love bashing skulls with mallets and tying intestines into knots."

"I didn't know that *specifically*, but..." She sighs, her shoulders dropping. "Jude, I'm serious. It's not worth it. Risking your cover, your lives... What if you get caught? What if you get hurt?"

"As long as I take those bastards down first, it's *all* worth it." My claws tighten possessively around her hips, and I suck in a deep breath, no longer able to keep up with the teasing and sarcasm—not about this. "Look, scarecrow. I'm not good at this shit. Words and feelings and trying to make sense of the shit in my head... It's a right mess. All I know is I need to take care of you, okay? I need to bloody take care of you because those fucking monsters didn't, and your fucking piece of shit father and stepmother didn't, and none of this shit should've *ever* happened to you. It fucking guts me. Absolutely fucking *guts* me, thinking of you like that... helpless and in pain and scared... It's eating me up inside. And yeah, I know I'm making this about what I need instead of what you need, and maybe I'm a selfish arsehole for it, but fuck it. I *am* selfish when it comes to you, and no, I won't walk away from this. I can't. I just... I just fucking can't." My voice breaks on the last words, my throat tight from holding back the roar in my chest, my heart slamming against my ribs, and if I try to hold her now, I'll fucking crush her with the force of everything I feel for her.

It's her gentle touch on my wings that drags me back from the brink, her palms stroking the crests.

"Jude," she says. "I get it. I get it, and if I can't stop you, then... Okay. Whatever you need to do? Get it done."

"You... you're saying you're actually okay with this now?"

She nods. "But I have one condition."

"Name it," I whisper.

She kisses me again, vicious and deep, fucking *devas-*

tating, and when she finally pulls back to meet my gaze, her blue-green eyes are damn near on fire with determination. "I'm going with you."

I skim my palms up her rib cage, thumbs brushing her nipples, making her gasp. "Scarecrow, when I find them, I'm not going to be kind."

"Skull-bashing, intestine-tying, bone-carving... Pretty sure you've set the scene for me, Jude. Clearly."

"Then *clearly* you can trust me and Augs to get the job done proper. You don't need to see us doing it."

"I've already seen you doing it, Jude. You slit Randall's throat right in front of me, remember?" She grins at me again, but it's no longer the sweet, innocent smile I've come to associate with our little witch. This one is brutal and cold and terribly hungry for something she hasn't even tasted yet.

This one is unhinged.

Something hot and fluttery swirls inside my chest, like my soul's just recognized its long-lost mate.

"Hmm." I drag a claw along her lower lip, back and forth. "Seems my little scarecrow *likes* watching me spill the blood of her enemies, doesn't she?"

"You have *no* idea." Pure, uncut lust darkens her eyes, and the scent of her desire spikes hard, heat radiating from between her thighs, making me *rock* fucking hard in an instant.

"I can smell your sweet little cunt, darling," I whisper,

my own grin turning feral. "That gives me a *very* good idea. Really sets the scene, as you say. And now I'm afraid you've left me no choice but to fucking *devour* you."

CHAPTER TEN

JUDE

I shove Randall's kneecaps aside and lay her on the table, ripping off her shorts and shredding the silky blue panties with the swipe of a single claw.

She opens her pretty little mouth to scold me, but I press that claw to her lips, silencing her.

"I've already taken the liberty of ordering you new undergarments, darling. Lots of them, in every color of the rainbow, so I can keep shredding them off you whenever the mood strikes. All that's left for you to decide is whether you want the sweatshirt to stay on tonight."

At first she shakes her head—an automatic response. But then she sighs and says, "Wait, no. I'm good. I want it off."

"You sure?"

With an emphatic nod, she unzips it and slides her arms out to unwrap herself for me, her perfect tits on full display.

I take a moment to admire the view, all smooth skin and soft curves, black-and-silver hair fanning out beneath her, lips parted as her chest rises and falls with ever-quickening breaths.

"Well, well, well. Aren't *you* a fine meal, all prepared for me on the breakfast table." Ditching my loincloth, I climb on top and lower my mouth to a dark pink nipple, flicking it with my tongue. Westlyn arches her back and grabs my horns, thighs parting, that soaking wet little cunt of hers already begging for it.

"Jude," she breathes, determined to keep me in a state of complete arousal for the rest of my fucking life. "Wait. What if we get caught?"

"Don't pretend you don't *want* to get caught, my little exhibitionist." I move to the other mouthwatering tit, sucking her nipple between my lips and grazing it with my fangs. "Be honest. You love putting on a show for your gargoyles, don't you?"

"Y-yes," she whispers. "Oh, goddess... Your mouth..."

"This mouth?" I tease, kissing a hot path down to her belly button. Then, gripping her thighs and spreading her wider, I swirl the tip of my tongue around her clit, the taste of her unleashing a deep growl inside me. "Mmm. You taste too fucking good, darling."

Burying my face between her thighs, I extend my tongue, tracing the outline of her lips before dipping inside, then dragging it back up to her clit, making her moan.

Fuck me, the way this girl writhes for me...

"Any pain after last night?" I whisper, retracting my claws and slowly slipping a finger inside her, then another.

"No, I... Auggie... He..." She trails off, her cheeks turning the color of the ripest apples in the orchard.

"Auggie *what*," I tease, giving her clit another lick as my fingers continue working her. "No secrets, remember?"

She swallows hard, her hips arching up, clearly desperate for more of my touch, my kiss. "He... he helped me feel better."

"I see." In and out, my fingers glide, spreading her, teasing her, getting her ready for more of me. Fucking *all* of me. "And *how* did he help you feel better?"

"Um... in lots of... different ways."

"I'm afraid you'll need to be more specific. I want to know *exactly* what Augustine did to heal the ache between your thighs." I suck her clit between my lips.

Westlyn shivers. "He... He... touched me."

Sliding my fingers back inside, slow and deep, I whisper, "Did he touch you here? Like this?"

"No, with his mouth. And his... his tail."

Her breath hitches adorably on the word *tail*, and I can't help but smile.

Still a bit shy about how much you like the tail, huh? Let's see if we can fix that...

"And this... *tail* you're blushing over..." I bring my own tail up between her legs, lightly slapping her clit. "Did it touch you like this?"

"Not exactly the same way, but... *holy hell*. That's... that's nice, too."

"I've never been the competitive sort, but I can't have you giving Auggie *all* the credit. Besides, we're *both* responsible for your ravishing last night." I stroke her now, teasing her clit with the tip of my tail, my fingers pumping faster inside her. "That means we have an ongoing responsibility to make sure you're feeling very, *very* good."

"How very, *very* noble of—oh, fuck, Jude. That's... don't stop."

"I won't, darling. Not until you're coming all over my tail."

"No," she gasps. "Not like that. I want you inside me now. *Really* inside me. I can't wait another second. Please."

I let out a soft chuckle. So much for my grand plans of making her come all over my tail. But like I said earlier—I'll *never* say no to something that puts a smile like *that* on her pretty face.

"Lift your hips for me," I whisper, fisting my cock and teasing her entrance with the crown. "That's a good girl."

"Jude," she moans, and that's fucking it. I can't hold back. I bring one of her legs up over my shoulder, wrap my hand around her throat, and fucking *bury* myself.

She pulses around me, hot and needy as I fuck her, driving in fast, then pulling back in a slow, erotic tease, only to slam right back into her again. Again and again and again, and all the while, my little scarecrow takes it.

Loves it.

Fucking *needs* it, her soft moans filling the kitchen, her eyes wild, skin slick beneath my touch, heartbeat throbbing and oh *fuck* how I want to keep giving it to her, just like this. One deep thrust at a time.

"Don't stop," she demands, clutching my forearm while I squeeze her throat.

And I—more than eager to keep that blush on her skin, that smile on her lovely face—obey.

I unfurl my tongue, teasing her clit while I fuck her senseless on the table, the bones of the dead rattling beside us, the table legs scraping against the floor, and there's no fucking *way* I'll ever be able to eat a meal here again without remembering *this* fine dining experience.

It doesn't take long for us both to reach the precipice, her eyes closed, her back arched, my balls slapping her arse with every roll of my hips.

"Say my name," I whisper, slowing my thrusts just enough to feel her soft, wet heat clench around my dick. "Let me see it on your pretty little mouth."

"Jude," she breathes, her lips making that oh-so-perfect pout, and then I've got my tongue between her thighs again and I'm sliding back inside her and she's gone, just fucking gone, coming with a shudder so intense it makes her teeth chatter, her whole body vibrating and dragging me right down with her.

The hot tingling starts in my balls, spiraling out until I'm trembling with the force of it, coming inside her as she grips my horns and bucks her hips and says my name over and over with the softest little moans until I'm finally spent and panting.

I lower her leg from over my shoulder and collapse on top of her, breathing in the scent of her skin, her sweat, her hot breath stirring my hair.

I'd stay here all night if I could, but I don't want to smother the poor thing, so I shift back to give her some room and drag my mouth back down to my favorite spot. She's hot and wet and filthy because of me, and *fuck*, I can't get enough...

"I'm addicted to you, scarecrow. Getting to be a real problem, that. Tell you the truth, if I could suck my own cock, I'd do it just to get one more taste of this divine little cunt." I swirl my tongue around her sensitive clit, making her gasp and shudder all over again. "Do you remember what I told you about sleeping arrangements?"

Smiling, she says, "You wanted me in your bed. But we were already in Auggie's room last night and the sun was coming up and I just sort of... passed out."

"I know," I say softly. "And I let you stay put because you were all worn out and needed the rest, but *that* was a one-time concession. I want you in *my* bed this morning. Naked. Wet. Touching yourself while you think of me." Kissing my way back up to her ear, I nip her earlobe and whisper, "I want you making such a fine mess in my sheets that when the sun sets and I come down from the rooftop to fuck you awake, your scent is *everywhere*. Understand?"

"Yes," she whispers, and I slide my mouth to hers,

capturing that smile with a kiss. Doesn't last long though—interrupted by a rude string of curses from across the kitchen. We turn our heads—Westlyn gasping, me grinning—to see Draegan looming in the entryway, doing his best to appear even more smug and pissed off than usual.

But if the sudden bulge beneath his loincloth isn't already a dead giveaway, that look in his eyes sure is.

He's not mad. He's flustered and hot and turned on beyond reason, and if he wasn't so busy trying to maintain his semblance of control, he might actually have a little fun once in a while.

"Why hello, Draegan," I say while the poor girl turns red beneath me. "Fancy a bite to eat?"

CHAPTER ELEVEN

DRAEGAN

"It's not enough to request her scent on your sheets? You need it all over the kitchen table as well? Fucking Jude." I stalk past the pair on my way to the coffeemaker, then change my mind and go for the new bottle of cognac I stashed in the pantry instead. It's the equivalent of day drinking, but the way this night is starting? I fucking need it.

"Draegan," Jude says, grinning up at me with his glistening mouth, not bothering to climb off the girl he so clearly just feasted upon. "Is that any way to speak to my dining companion?"

Naked beneath him, Westlyn covers her face, muttering something about not wanting to get caught after all.

"Too late for regrets now, Miss Avery," I say. "That particular bell cannot be un-rung. You *can*, however, put your clothes back on. In fact, I insist."

Keeping his wild eyes locked on mine, Jude slides off and gets to his feet, offering a hand to help her off the table.

She hops down and scrambles to put on her sweatshirt and shorts. Where her undergarments ended up is a mystery I won't be solving anytime soon.

I down the first shot, then tip my empty glass toward the desecrated table. "That table is an original antique farmhouse piece hand-crafted in the eighteen hundreds."

"Ah! That explains why it's so sturdy." Jude pounds a fist on the table, then grips the edge and gives it a good shake. "Times like this, you really appreciate the craftsmanship of a thing. Think the Ikea version could take a pounding like that?"

I pour another drink and lift it to my lips. "Didn't think Miss Avery could either," I mutter into the glass.

"Watch your tone, Draegan," Jude says. He's still smiling, but the threat in his eyes is clear.

"My apologies." I down the drink and glare right back at him. Five minutes in the same room, and I'm already exhausted by his antics. "Now if you don't mind, Jude, I've got a few things to discuss with Miss Avery. Privately."

"Wait, you're talking to me now?" she asks. "After dropping me on my ass and slamming the door in my face last night?"

"It would seem so, yes."

"You're not going to pick me up and throw me out in the yard, are you?"

"Not if you behave yourself."

"And if I don't?" She folds her arms over her chest, eyes blazing, the momentary embarrassment she suffered suddenly vanishing. "Because let's face it, *Daddy* Drae, you've got a lot of rules and regulations lately. Kinda hard for a girl to keep track."

I take a step closer, gazing down into her eyes, at her heat-stained cheeks, at the lips swollen from Jude's hungry kiss, desperately willing the memories of last night's shower session out of my mind...

Let me come, Daddy. Please...

"*Do* try to be on your best behavior, little mortal," I say firmly, forcing the inappropriate thoughts out of my mind, which is no easy feat, what with the damn *scent* of her lingering all around me. "Tonight is *not* the night to tempt fate."

We continue staring each other down, neither of us giving an inch. It's become our usual dance, but it doesn't bode well for the conversation we're about to have.

I reach for the bottle again.

Getting through this unscathed is going to require a good deal of patience, a heaping dose of tact, and a hell of a lot more booze.

"Jude," I say again, still not looking away from Westlyn. "Don't you have a meeting with Augustine?"

"It can wait," he says, wrapping a protective arm over her shoulders.

"It's fine," Westlyn says, finally turning those fiery eyes away from me to gaze *adoringly* at the other gargoyle.

For fucks's sake, that really shouldn't bother me as much as it does.

I pour another drink.

"Seriously, Jude," Westlyn says. "I'm pretty sure Draegan and I can manage to get through one conversation without killing each other."

"He's immortal, darling. Hardly a fair fight."

"Don't underestimate me, gargoyle." She throws a playful punch into his chest, but before she connects, he grabs her fist and kisses her knuckles.

"Never," he says, grinning at her like a lovesick fool. Then, turning to me with a look that's decidedly *not* lovesick, "Behave yourself, Draegan. Or you and I will be having the sort of conversation that *does* involve killing."

"Before you say anything," I say the minute Westlyn returns from the bathroom, "I owe you an apology."

She stops in her tracks and blinks at me as if she doesn't recognize the gargoyle standing before her. "Is this a trap? This feels like a trap."

"More like a peace offering." I hand over the almond joy latte I just made—rather, *attempted* to make—and gesture toward the stools at the countertop, inviting her to sit. "Last night in my suite, I let my temper get the better of me, and I'm sorry. It won't happen again."

She laughs, taking the offered drink with a wary glance

at the contents. "You sure about that? You and your temper seem to be in a bit of a co-dependent relationship."

"Careful, Miss Avery," I tease. "Or I might start to think you *like* pushing me to my breaking point."

"Who, me? This picture of wholesome innocence right here?" She circles her face with a finger and laughs again, and I can't help but smile back, the earlier tension between us finally loosening up. "Okay," she continues, "maybe you're a *tiny* bit right. I swear I used to be the most docile girl on the planet. But ever since the whole demonic wedding disaster, it seems I'm having some minor authority—"

"Issues," I supply.

"I was going to say challenges, but fine. Issues works." Her laughter finally fades. "Hey. I'm sorry, too, Draegan. I know I can be... stubborn sometimes. And I totally appreciate what you're doing for me—all of you. It can't be easy having a houseguest."

That's putting it mildly...

"It also can't be easy living with four overbearing gargoyles," I concede.

"What? Living here is a cakewalk. Only one of you is overbearing. Not to name names or anything."

I wink at her across the countertop. "Probably for the best."

She finally takes a sip of the latte. Her nose crinkles, but she nods in appreciation. "It's... different. But good. In its own special Draegan way."

"Not in an almond joy latte way, then?"

"You get an A for effort, but... no. Not even close." She laughs and takes another sip. "We'll call this one... I know! Daddy Drae's Delight."

Not for the first time in her presence, I'm more than grateful for the countertop between us, blocking the view of my twitching cock.

"Cheers, then." I touch my cocktail glass to her mug and down another shot, hoping the alcohol dims the echo of her words.

Because Daddy Drae's *real* delight isn't a coffee drink at all. It's her, naked and on her knees, mascara-stained tears leaking down her cheeks as she chokes on my cock...

I close my eyes and think of the sea, the rolling hills of old, the cold winter winds, and we sit together in silence for a few moments—her, comfortable and content. Me, aching and annoyed.

But then she says, "So, was there something else you wanted to talk about, or was this truly just a peace offering?"

I open my eyes, reality sweeping back in like that cruel winter wind.

"It's truly a peace offering, but yes, there's... something else." I pour another shot, but leave the glass untouched as I search for the least painful way to bring this up. "Miss Avery, I... You should know that... That is to say I... There's something..." I pinch the bridge of my nose and whisper a curse, wishing I had a handbook for this. The last thing I want to do is fumble my words and hurt her or make her feel like she can't trust the others, but I have to get this out.

I need her to know that I know about her past. Her scars. The terror that still plagues her nightmares no matter how much so-called "nocturnal reframing" she attempts.

I need her to know that it's okay. That we're all here for her, in whatever way she needs us.

And as hard as it is to admit, *I* need to know that *she's* okay.

Taking a deep breath, I force myself to meet her gaze once more. "Augustine... He told me about what you went through as a child."

"I... Oh." She lowers her gaze, her cheeks darkening ever so slightly.

"He only mentioned it because he and Jude are working with Rook to track down the perpetrators, and he wanted to inform me of their plans. They're going after shadow magic society mages, Miss Avery. It affects all of us."

"It's... it's fine," she says, staring into the mug as if she'd like to jump right in and disappear. "I told them I wasn't trying to keep it secret or anything."

"He mentioned that. I just... About what happened to you... I want you to know that I—"

She holds up a hand, silencing me. "Whatever you're about to say, I'm sure it's kind and coming with the best of intentions, and I appreciate it."

"It is, but—"

"Then let's leave it at that."

"Miss Avery, if you'll just—"

"Please, Draegan. I can't go there again." She finally lifts her gaze, her eyes glassy with unshed tears. "Not with you."

"Oh. I... I understand," I say, trying to ignore the jealous burn that seems intent on eating away at me tonight. "Of course. If you ever change your mind and want to talk about it, I'm—"

"Thanks for the latte. Can I go?"

"Not yet. I'm afraid there's one more thing we need to discuss." I down the cognac, the alcohol burning away the jealousy in my chest. "Your relationship with Jude."

CHAPTER TWELVE

DRAEGAN

So much for the peace offering.

"That's none of your business," she snaps, shattering our fragile truce. "What Jude and I have or don't have is strictly between us."

"I see. So having an early evening go-round on our community dining table... That's keeping things private, is it?"

"Wow. Just... wow." She shoves away the mug and hops up from the stool. "I should've known better than to trust an apology from you. Enjoy your evening, Draegan. Try not to choke on your self-righteousness."

Fuck.

"Miss Avery, wait. Please. I'm sorry—again. Just... just let me explain."

She pops her hands on her hips, bare foot tapping the floor, eyes narrowed like she's about to roast me with a glare. "Talk fast, gargoyle. You've got thirty seconds to convince me you're not a *complete* tool whose sole M.O. is hurting everyone who comes into your orbit."

"I just mean that Jude is... He's volatile. *Extremely* volatile. And he's fiercely loyal to those he cares about—especially to you. That combination makes him downright dangerous."

"No, that combination makes him someone I'm downright grateful to have in my corner. Aren't you?"

"Of course. It's just... He had a hard enough time making rational decisions and showing restraint before you came into our lives. Now? You're all he bloody talks about."

"Really?" She blushes again and flashes an unexpected smile, looking like a damn teenager with her first crush. "Like, what kinds of stuff does he say?"

"All manner of things that continue to convince me he's completely lost the ability to think clearly."

"You're something else, aren't you?" Her smile vanishes. "Don't you see how much he respects you? Looks up to you? Goddess, they all do. I've only been around you guys for a hot minute, but it's so obvious to me that the gargoyles would do anything for you."

"As would I, for them."

"Then how can you stand here criticizing Jude? Talking about him like he's an annoying, misbehaving kid who—"

"Jude is my brother in every way that matters, Miss Avery," I counter, my voice rising. "We have stood by each other for nearly a hundred times longer than you've even been alive. *Never* question my gratitude for him."

The little mortal is smart enough to wipe that condescending look off her face. In a slightly more contrite tone, she says, "If that's how you feel, then why are you lecturing me about how volatile he is?"

"Because that's just a part of who he is—a part you need to be aware of. And while his loyalty is commendable—and much appreciated, believe me—it also means he has a tendency to overreact and under-think. When it comes to eliminating threats against those he loves, Jude's rash behavior and consistently bad calls have put our organization in hot water with the human feds more times than I can count, and—"

"Oh, your *organization*," she says, making air quotes around the word. "Right. I keep forgetting what the priorities are here. For a split second there, I thought we were all about breaking the curse and taking down our mutual enemies. My bad! Phew! Thank the Morrigan you're here to keep me on task!"

"Those *are* the priorities, Miss Avery, but I can't focus on them if I'm stuck doing damage control after Jude's gone off on another bender."

"That's what you're calling it? A bender? He's planning to take down a pack of dark mages who terrorized me when we were kids, spent their adult years committing felonies and hurting who knows how many other women, have connections to the same society that planned to bind me to a demon, and you think that's a *bender?*"

"You know what I mean."

"No, Draegan. I really don't. Because as far as I can tell, he's just trying to follow through on the promises you made. Promises you haven't done a damn thing to—"

"What promises?"

"To keep me safe. To rid the world of the Forsythes and all the vile mages in their employ in exchange for my help stealing and translating the Cerridwen Codex. That was the deal, remember? So far, I've kept up my end of the bargain. Can you say the same?"

The fact that she'd ever question me on my word has my wings rippling with indignation.

I step out from behind the counter, crowding into her space, forcing her to tip her head back to meet my furious gaze.

In a dark voice, I say softly, "You think I'm reneging on our deal, little mortal?"

"I... I don't know. Are you?"

"You think I haven't been working tirelessly every waking hour—on top of all my other responsibilities—to ensure no harm comes to you? To build an airtight plan of attack against the Forsythes, against Zorakkov, against your parents, against every single attendee at that sham of a wedding?"

She lowers her chin and drops her gaze, but I'm not letting her off the hook so easily.

Gripping her jaw, I tilt her face up once more and lower my mouth to her ear, careful to enunciate every word. "Do *not* question my ability to do what needs to be done to ensure your longevity, little mortal. Promises are not a thing I make lightly. Not to my men. And most certainly not to you. Are we clear?"

"Yes," she whispers.

"What was that? I didn't quite hear you."

Heat swirls through her blue-green irises, and when she speaks again, her voice is firm. "*Yes.* We're clear."

I release her jaw and return to my spot behind the counter, eager for another drink. But my cognac glass is tipped on its side, two intruders sniffing around beside it.

"Great," I say, attempting to shoo the ravens off. "I hope you hellions at least had the decency to wipe your feet before making yourselves at home on my countertop."

"Don't yell at my birds." Westlyn reclaims her stool, reaching out to stroke one of the ravens' heads. "Ignore him, Luce. He's in a mood."

She's baiting me again, but I refuse to walk into her trap. The fact is, we need to finish this conversation. Jude can't afford to be distracted by his infatuation with her, and she needs to come to terms with that.

Before he gets us all into a situation we *can't* fix with bribes and threats.

"Miss Avery," I say, my voice even, "I'm simply trying to impress upon you the reality of our situation. We four are the only remaining living gargoyles. We're living double lives

—men and monsters both—and we walk a *very* delicate balance in this city. Jude's a risk—always has been. I've mitigated it for years, but with his feelings for you complicating things..." I let out a deep sigh, scratching one of the ravens between its wings. "I'm not trying to be indelicate here, nor will I attempt to dictate whose bed you share. I'm just asking you to see things from my perspective and trust that I'm only trying to do what's best. For my men *and* for you."

"You think I don't know that?"

"If you did, perhaps you'd try talking him out of this ridiculous vigilante mission."

"His little *bender*, you mean?"

"I'm not saying those mages don't deserve to die—and die horrifically, at that." My hand tightens around the bottle of cognac, knuckles whitening at the thought of her on those subway tracks. "But first, I think we all need to take a step back and comb through Rook's intel, fully assess the targets and risks, and come up with a better plan. It's a perfectly reasonable suggestion."

"I never said it wasn't. I just think—"

"It's a mystery to me, Miss Avery, why you always feel the need to disagree with me."

"It's a mystery to *me*, Mr. Caldwell, why you always feel the need to shut me down before I've even finished speaking."

"Perhaps I'm trying to stem another argument."

"Have you ever considered we might actually be on the same page? That we might finally find the common ground you were so adamant about when we first made our little deal, if only you'd... Never mind. Forget it."

"If only I'd what?" I press. "Don't hold back now, Miss Avery. We're finally making some progress."

"Fine. I was *going* to say, if only you'd try being less of a dick about things, but then I remembered it's literally *impossible* for you to be less of a dick. Dick is baked into your DNA, right along with those stormy eyes and that maddening—"

"The only thing *maddening* in this equation is *you*."

"And here we go again. Blame the new girl for all the things you've been fucking up on this earth for the last billion years."

I scoff. "I've hardly been on this earth a billion years."

"The other guys don't treat me like this, Draegan. This is definitely a *you* problem."

"That's because they're too busy making doe-eyes at you across the room, which is exactly how you like it, isn't it? A kiss here, a kiss there, bat your lashes and your wishes are their command."

"Actually, yeah. I *do* like that. A lot. In fact, I'll take their kisses and doe-eyes to your rudeness and icy dagger-eyes any day of the week."

"Quite pathetic, really, the way they follow you about. Are they vicious gargoyles, or little lost puppies in search of an available teat to suckle? Who can say?"

I don't mean it, of course. All their bedroom games and kitchen table dalliances aside, it's obvious the others are doing what they can to protect her and one another, inside this house and out.

But so am I. If anything is baked into my DNA, it's that—protectiveness. And here, in *this* century, in *this* realm, that protectiveness has manifested in an unshakeable *need* to keep her safe, regardless of how badly she drives me up the fucking walls.

Let me come, Daddy. Please...

"I don't know why I even bother trying to have a normal conversation with you," she snaps. "Fifteen minutes in the same room with you, and I'm ready to turn myself in and take my chances with the demon prince."

"Last I checked, there are several *thousand* square feet in this manor. Feel free to relocate yourself to any of them."

She laughs, harsh and bitter. "Why should I relocate when you're the one who sucks?"

"I'm just saying, it seems like the obvious solution when you *allegedly* can't stand being in the same room with someone."

"Allegedly?"

"Your smart little mouth says one thing, yet here you remain. Taunting me. Glaring at me. Perhaps you're infatuated with me."

"Perhaps *you're* infatuated with *me*."

"Not possible, I *assure* you."

"No?" She leans across the counter, her grin malicious. Then, her sugary sweet voice dripping with mock innocence, "So why are you rocking a hard-on for me?"

"What? You think that's *your* doing?" I huff and shake my head. "Typical. Everything is always about you, isn't it?"

"No one else is here but Lucinda and Huxley. So unless you've got an undisclosed bird fetish, then yeah, I'm taking full credit for the state of affairs between your legs."

"You tell yourself whatever you need to, love." I turn away from her and bring up my glamour, burying the monster inside the man.

It only makes her laugh again. "Oh, I see how it is."

"Glad to hear it. For a moment there, I thought I'd need to draw you a diagram." Turning back toward her, glamour firmly in place, I make a dismissive gesture toward the entryway. "Run along now, little mortal. The grown-ups have work to do."

"Whatever." She hops off the stool, bare feet slapping against the floor. "I'm going to the library to check on Rook."

"You do that."

"Happily."

"Good."

"*Double* good," she snaps. "And in the meantime, you can go... I don't know. Prepare for a call with the commissioner or polish your fancy briefcase or whatever other *grown-up* things need doing."

She marches away, her birds hopping along behind her, the lingering scent of her desire wrapping me in an invisible choke-hold.

When she reaches the entryway, she turns to look at me

over her shoulder, that malicious grin touching her lips again. "Oh, and Draegan?"

For fuck's sake...

"What now?" I bark.

Her eyes rove down my body, stopping right on my still-hard, still-aching cock. Human, yes, but no less obvious.

"I think your glamour's broken," she says, again with the saccharine-sweet innocence. "Is it supposed to be sticking out like that? I mean, not to make you self-conscious or anything, but that looks *super* uncomfortable."

And with a final know-it-all smirk, the little brat turns on her heel and marches out, once again leaving me to contemplate whether I should ignore her completely, put her out on her arse, or chase her down, throw her over my knee, and spank her until she's begging me to finally fuck that smart little mouth into submission.

CHAPTER THIRTEEN

ROOK

After spending the first part of the evening compiling all the intel on the mages who hurt West, I'm more than ready to get back to work on the Cerridwen Codex. The book itself remains one of the most challenging unsolved mysteries we've ever encountered, but my approach to cracking the code is a familiar comfort.

And right now, if there's anything that can take my mind off the atrocities our little witch endured, it's the ever-reliable scientific method.

I've done the research. Formulated my questions and hypotheses. Made a few initial observations. But we still haven't been able to open the damn thing.

So my next order of business? Reviewing the feeds on the new security cams I set up in the library last night. The Codex continues to exhibit strange physical properties whenever one of us touches it—a faint purple glow emanating from the cover, alternating flashes of black and purple sparks, an occasional electrical humming noise.

So far, West is the only one experiencing actual headaches, but the other effects are common to all who've handled it, starting with the first moment Drae plucked it off Lennon Forsythe's shelf.

What I'm hoping to determine now is whether those same observable behaviors—or any others, for that matter—occur at random, when no one's causing any external physical stimulus.

Queuing up the camera feed on my tablet, I settle into a chair by the crackling fire, prop my feet up on the ottoman, and hit the play button on the recording from last night.

I watch for a few minutes, then kick up the playback speed, confirming my initial assumptions—no observable visual or aural phenomenon.

But a couple of hours into the recording, things finally start to get interesting.

West shows up.

After another failed attempt to open the Codex— including the expected electrical jolt and ensuing adorable yelp—she gives the thing the middle finger and settles into her chair with a book on gargoyle lore. I don't speed through this part—I love watching her read, her eyes shining with curiosity, a tiny wrinkle of concentration between her eyebrows. She's humming softly, too—I'm not even sure she realizes she's doing it.

I'm still not sure why fate brought her into our lives,

but *fuck*... Watching her in the library, her feet tucked under her, that soft tune floating on the air... I can't help but feel like she's always been part of us. Our fifth, even without the wings and tail. We waited fifteen hundred years before she crashed onto the scene, but after just a couple of short weeks, I can't imagine our lives without her.

No matter how many years—or how few—we've got left.

I hear the door open on the recording, and then she's glancing at the entryway, her face lighting up as Auggie crosses the room.

"I see we're still in hiding," he says with a smirk, taking a seat on the couch across from her. "It won't help, you know. He can scent you. All of us can."

"Thanks for the hot tip," she says with her patented eye roll. "Anyway. If by *he* you're referring to the grump formerly known as Daddy Drae, then yes. I'm hiding from him."

While the two of them chat a bit about Draegan and the Codex, and get in a good deal of flirting while they're at it, I head into the kitchen to clean my glasses and whip up a latte, leaving the tablet on the countertop beside me.

It takes me two tries to get the foam right, and the final product isn't anywhere near as good as Stella's or even Auggie's, but hey. It's hot and sweet and just the pick-me-up I need.

By the time I put on my glasses and grab the tablet again, it's clear I missed a whole lot. Last I knew, they were talking about the Codex and the curse, but the scene has most definitely... *progressed*.

Now, it's not the Codex causing an electrical jolt.

It's Auggie. And West. And... *hot damn*.

I barely manage to set down the latte without dropping it.

West is in his lap, writhing against his hand as he fingers her with deep, slow thrusts...

"Fuck," Auggie hisses, very quickly losing himself. "You're already so wet for me, witchling. So eager."

I stare at the screen, my drink all but forgotten as she strokes his horns, her soft little moans encouraging him to bring her right to the edge, closer and closer, and then...

Fuck...

Suddenly she's on her knees for him, reaching under his loincloth to stroke him with both hands, her fingers small and delicate as they struggle to hold that massive gray cock...

No. I shouldn't be watching this. I need to shut it down, delete the evidence, pretend I never saw it, and get back to work on the Codex, but...

Holy shit. I am *definitely* going to hell. There's no hope for me. Not a fucking chance. Because now she's licking him, sucking him, taking him into that hot little mouth while Auggie fists her hair and fucks her, just the way he wants her.

"You're... you're killing me, witchling," he growls. "Fucking *killing* me."

This is wrong. Wrong, wrong, *wrong* but it's too late. I'm already zooming in on the footage, my free hand snaking beneath my loincloth and fisting my cock, my eyes glued to the screen as I stroke myself to the soundtrack of her sweet little moans and Auggie's deep, rich commands, her kisses growing more fevered and sloppy, his control unraveling...

"Westlyn, *fuck*..." he grinds out. "That's it. Right there. *Right* fucking—"

"Auggie? That you?" comes the melodic call, and no, it's not from the feed.

I drop the tablet and knock over the latte, glancing up just in time to catch West bouncing into the kitchen, her smile bright, Lucinda and Huxley plodding along behind her.

"If you're making lattes," she sing-songs, "I'll let you touch my boobs if you share with—oh, shit! *Rook?* Oh, *goddess*! I thought you were Auggie!"

We lock eyes, her mouth parted in a gasp, sweatshirt hanging off her shoulders, her perfect breasts bared as the shock of finding me here freezes her on the spot. My heart lodges in my throat, my cock still hard and throbbing as the security footage drones on obliviously, filling the awkward silence with Auggie's final command...

"I let you have *your* fun," he rasps. "Now it's my turn. And *my* fun involves throwing you down and fucking you the way I've been dreaming about fucking you every goddamn night since I first saw you in that lacy black dress."

I watch as the realization dawns, staining her cheeks red. Those big blue-green eyes widen, and a soft gasp rushes through her parted lips. Spinning away from me, she pulls her sweatshirt back on and yanks the zipper all the way up.

But she doesn't make a move to leave. Not one single step.

"How did you..." she breathes. "Where did you get that video?"

"There are security cameras in the main library room, West." The admission burns through my chest.

"What?" She turns back to look at me, confusion written plainly on her face. "Since when?"

"I'm so, so sorry. I installed the system to keep an eye on the Codex, and completely forgot to mention it. This is the first I've even checked the footage—I wanted to get a full night's worth to see if there were any patterns in the book's behavior. I didn't realize you'd been in here with Auggie last night—I mean, I knew you'd been *in* here, physically speaking, but not in that *specific* physical and highly intimate sort of way with all the touching and the..." I clear my throat and duck her gaze, desperately willing my cock to go back into hiding.

But she's not letting me off the hook.

"And?" she presses, hands on her hips. "Did you find what you were looking for?"

"No, I... I... I was scanning through the feed and suddenly there you were, in his lap, like..." I feel my cock stiffening again, and I close my eyes, trying to shove those memories out of my skull. "I should've turned it off. Immediately. But I kept telling myself just one more second, and before I knew it I was just... You're just so wild and beautiful and you guys were *sooo* into each other and I couldn't stop watching and I know it was a complete and utter violation of your trust, and please, please, *please* tell me what I can do to fix this. Anything. Name it and it's done."

She's still glaring at me—I can feel the heat of her scrutiny raking over my bare chest. Hear the frantic beat of her heart thrumming wildly inside her. Hear the soft, ragged breaths in time with the rise and fall of her shoulders.

Steadying myself, I take a deep breath.

The scent of her desire is potent and unmistakable.

And when I finally find the courage to look her in the eyes again, she's smiling so big and bright, she's barely holding back a laugh.

"Are you... laughing at me right now?" I let out a chuckle of my own, grateful for the levity but completely confused. "Seriously? You're not upset? Or are you one of those people who laughs during moments of heightened emotion, in which case, once again, I'm so sorry for—"

"Has anyone ever told you... You're rather adorable when you're rambling and embarrassed?"

Fresh heat rushes to my cheeks, my glasses slipping down my nose. "I... I don't think I've *ever* rambled this much. Or been this embarrassed, for that matter. Not as a mortal *or* a gargoyle."

"First time for everything, huh?" she teases.

I try to hold my grin, but a wave of hot, fresh guilt washes through my gut, making me wince. She's taking it all in stride, but still. "West, I... There's no excuse for what I did. My actions were... I can't apologize enough. Truly. I'm completely ashamed."

"Don't be. It's okay."

"No, it isn't. I don't want you to feel like you don't have any privacy, or worry that I don't respect you. I promise I do. I'm just a complete and utter creep who—"

"Rook. Honestly?" She pads into the kitchen on soft footfalls, her scent swirling around me. Then, stretching up on her toes to trace her fingertips along my beard, she whispers, "I kind of like it. *Really* like it, actually."

I swallow hard, my heart thudding, my throat tight. "Really like what?"

"Being watched like that. By you, I mean." She slides her palms down my chest, fingers hooking into the top of my loincloth, her soft touch stirring my cock to life all over again.

"Westlyn," I growl, not entirely sure whether it's a warning or a promise, but her fingers are brushing against my bare skin and she's so warm and sweet and she's standing so, so fucking close...

"I know this sounds a little nutty," she says softly, then laughs. "Well, maybe no more nutty than the fact that gargoyles are real and we're investigating dark mages and a fae curse and a witch whose father tried to pawn her off to a demon prince, but..." She sighs, warm breath misting across my chest. "I care about you guys. All four of you. Yes, even Draegan, despite his endless crankiness."

I cup her cheek, damn close to losing myself in her eyes. "We care about you, too, West. You have to know that."

"I *do* know that. I guess what I'm trying to say is… Rook, I love hanging out with you. I love our chats and study sessions, I love when you teach me about gargoyle and fae lore, and I'd never want to do anything to jeopardize that. But you obviously know I've been… intimate with Auggie, and you've probably figured out it's the same way with Jude, and…"

"And what?"

"Depending on how you feel, I'd be open to… to exploring things with you, too. Like, more-than-friend things. *Physical* more-than-friend things, and oh my goddess, please shove a book into my hands and give me an assignment so I can finally stop talking before I completely obliterate the last of my dignity."

"And keep all the rambling embarrassment to myself? Never." I laugh, then run a hand over her head, tugging on one of her silver locks. "We should probably get to work."

She grins up at me, her eyes sparkling, fingers still curled around the top of my loincloth. "You sure?"

My thoughts come fast and furious.

No, beautiful. The only thing I'm sure about is how badly I want to strip you bare, lay you out on the library table, and film you playing with your pretty little pussy until you come all over your fingers, moaning for me like a wild thing…

But out loud, I say only, "I'm... sure."

I break away from her and busy myself cleaning up the drink I spilled, which has now made a colossal mess all over the counter. Better that way, though—gives me time to put the proverbial leash on this ridiculous hard-on.

Westlyn's offer is *beyond* tempting.

But... no. I can't. Right now, my only job is to crack the code on the Codex, figure out why the Forsythes and her parents were so bent on binding her to that demon, and determine how the two things are connected. Her very life depends on my ability to think clearly, and I can't do that if I'm using our time together to indulge in my fantasies.

Fantasies that are more depraved than our naughty little witch could ever imagine...

"So what's on the agenda tonight, Professor Peepshow?" she asks, rummaging in the cupboard for some cheese crackers for the ravens.

Shooting her a teasing, don't-get-me-started glare, I say, "Demonology. I dug up a few more seminary works on our dastardly prince of hell—thought we could do a deep dive."

She pumps her fist in the air. "You always plan the *best* date nights."

"You say that now, but that's only because you haven't seen how long these articles are. Seminary students like to wax poetic about all sorts of things, and you, my little over-achiever, are on highlighter duty." I toss the spent rag into the sink and turn the coffee machine back on. "You still want that latte?"

"Depends." She grins at me, all mischievous and adorable again, and tugs at the top of her zipper. "You gonna cash in on the offer to touch my boobs?"

"Oh, absolutely." I grab her wrist, pulling it away from the zipper and pressing a kiss to her fingertips. Then, with a grin and a wink, "But not tonight, Wild West. Now stop trying to distract me, and get to work."

CHAPTER FOURTEEN

ROOK

While Lucinda and Huxley take turns stashing cheese crackers in every nook and cranny in the library, West and I spend the next few hours poring over the seminary texts, bouncing theories back and forth about the demon Zorakkov's grand plans for manifestation.

According to the lore, many hellbound demons have a desire at some point in their eternal lives to fully incarnate on the earthly realm and expand their domains—a goal that requires a series of human vessels and a coven of dark witches or mages willing to summon them, bind them to the first vessel, and relinquish the power they'd otherwise retain over a demon they summoned with their own dark magic.

Of course, any magic user who'd willingly summon a demon like Zorakkov in the first place isn't going to be the most trustworthy sort, which is why powerful demons rarely achieve their manifestation goals. Ninety-nine-point-nine percent of the time, they end up enslaved to the coven or worse—trapped in the void between realms because their human vessel dies and the coven doesn't reappoint another one to serve in its place.

When they do manage to break free of a coven's bond? Chaos ensues. A demon strong enough to break the spell that summoned them will often unleash hell—pun intended—in a massive burst of power, but it burns out fast. Within days, maybe a week at most. Then they find themselves right back where they started—wandering around in hell with their tail up their ass, waiting for the next desperate coven with a summoning spell.

Right now, we know Zorakkov is possessing Hunter Forsythe's body. We *don't* know how long he's been here, how long he's got left, what the shadow magic society stands to gain out of the deal, and most importantly—why the hell they're all so desperate to bind him to our witch.

"I need a caffeine refill—my eyes are glazing over." West gets to her feet and stretches, her sweatshirt riding up to reveal her smooth, bare stomach. "You want another round?"

Forcing myself to stare long and hard at the text spread out before me, I nod. "But I'll get them—you relax. What would you like? Another almond joy?"

"Sit down, sit down." She skims her hand along the tips of my wings as she passes, and it's all I can do not to shiver. "No offense, Rook, but you make a better professor than a barista. Now tell me your order or you're stuck with what-ever mad scientist concoction I come up with."

She returns a few minutes later with two frothy soy pepper-mint mochas—a departure from her usual—and a little more pep in her step. Still, tonight's endless theorizing is clearly wearing on her—her eyes are rimmed in red, and she's barely holding back a yawn.

"Hey. You feeling okay?" I ask, taking the mugs from her hands and setting them on the table. "We can stop if you'd like, come back fresh tomorrow night. I know some of this reading is pretty dry."

"No, it's not the reading. It's that damn Codex." She heads over to the other table where the Codex has been parked since Drae and I so expertly purloined it from Forsythe's brownstone. As soon as she draws near, the whole thing lights up, black and purple sparks zipping along its surface. "See? I didn't even have to touch it this time. I swear the damn thing has it out for me."

"Wow. That's new, huh?"

"Yep." She glares at it and rolls her eyes. "Okay, asshole. You don't like me—message received. The feeling is *more* than mutual."

"What about the headaches?"

She rubs her temples. "I've been trying to ignore it since I walked in here tonight, but no dice."

"Does it still feel like someone's hammering away inside your head?"

"Oh, they're done hammering. Now it just feels like they're trying to straight-up erase whatever's left inside."

"What do you mean?"

Returning to our table, she wraps her hands around the mug and takes a long drink. "It almost reminds me of an allergy. That pressure feeling? And the brain fog... You know, now that we're talking about it, it's a lot like my stupid wedding bouquet—goddess, I was so out of it that night."

"What's the story with the bouquet?"

"That thing was cursed—I swear. Eloise picked it out, and as soon as the florist dropped it off, I was already sneezing and coughing like crazy. Luce didn't like it either—gave the thing a wide berth. I thought I was allergic, so I tried to give it away to the girl at the hotel desk, hoping some beautiful flowers would brighten her night. But when Eloise found out, she completely freaked."

She tells me the rest of the story—how Eloise forced her to carry it down the aisle, her head finally starting to clear when she set it on the altar. And then, finally, how the damn thing went up in a blaze of glory when her birds swooped down and knocked over the altar candles.

"The instant those flowers burned," she says, "I knew—with a shocking burst of clarity—that the mage I was about to bind myself to wasn't a mage at all, but a demon. It was like the fog just evaporated, and that's when I saw his black demon eyes and heard his voice in my head. His name. *Zorakkov.*"

West tugs her sleeves down over her hands, wrapping her arms around herself like she's suddenly cold.

I rise and toss another log onto the fire. "And that's what you're feeling now? That same kind of fog?"

"Pretty much. It's like a low-level static in my head. Like, the more time I spend in here, the harder my thoughts are to follow. It's not as intense as the flowers, but similar."

"Do you remember which flowers were in the bouquet?"

"Roses and peonies, but I've never been allergic to those. There were also these tiny silver bell-type flowers, and a bunch of random greenery."

"Silver bells? How tiny?"

"About the size of a pea. Oh, and they had black tips, almost like the bells were dipped in ink. They were super pretty, but I couldn't really enjoy them."

Damn it.

"Sit tight, West," I say. "I've got a theory."

CHAPTER FIFTEEN

ROOK

I fly up to the loft, scanning the shelves for a reference book I was working with a few weeks back. Silver bells dipped in ink... I swear I came across an illustration of flowers matching that exact description...

I finally find it—an old, leather-bound tome called *Flora and Fauna of Ancient Faerie.*

"Check this out." I glide back down and flip through the book until I find the two-page spread detailing the flowers —Midnight's Lullaby, they're called. "Are these the ones from your bouquet?"

West comes around to my side of the table and leans in close, her long hair sweeping over my shoulder. "Yep, that's them. Exactly."

"You're certain?"

"Positive. They're so lovely. I'd never admit this to Eloise, but I was actually kind of bummed they didn't agree with my system." She traces a fingertip over the sketch, reading the description. "Midnight's Lullaby... Even the name is pretty. Too bad they were trying to murder me."

"Not murder you, West." I close the book and meet her gaze. "Midnight's Lullaby is indigenous to Faerie—it's nearly impossible to find in this realm. Whoever got it for your bouquet must've smuggled it in—the fae have been trying to eradicate it from their own lands for millennia."

"Why is it so forbidden?"

"In large enough doses, the pollen can be toxic to fae. In small doses, however, it merely dampens their inherent magic."

"Wait... But that's... What are you saying? That I'm definitely fae?"

"We knew it was a possibility, given your reaction to Zorakkov's blood. Now, hearing how you reacted to these flowers—"

"But I don't have any magic. There's nothing to dampen."

"You might not have any *witch* magic, and the fae blood you inherited might be very, very watered down at this point. But even a trace amount would've caused a reaction. The symptoms you described are all signs of a body's inherent magic mounting a defense against a perceived threat, just like your immune system does with a virus or infection. And you said it yourself—the moment the ravens destroyed the flowers, you could sense the demon. Anyone with fae blood would've sensed a demonic presence immediately—their magic can detect it."

"Wow." She goes to stand near the fire, her back to me, the firelight casting her in a golden halo. In a soft voice, she says, "So it's true, then. I *do* have dark fae blood in me, just as you guys suspected."

"There's no doubt in my mind."

"Does that mean... Am I dark, too?" She turns to look at me again, her face pinched with worry.

"No more than someone who's great-great-great cousin-once-removed committed a murder. That has nothing to do with who or what you are, West. Only *you* get to decide that."

It's a long moment before she speaks again, and when she does, her voice is barely a whisper. "She knew, Rook. Eloise knew."

"About your fae lineage?"

"Why else would she have gone to so much trouble over the flowers? She must've known I was at least some part fae, and she couldn't risk me figuring out Hunter was possessed by a demon. It would've thrown off the whole plan."

"Well, turns out she was right. It *did* throw off the whole plan. With a little help from your ravens, you figured it out, and you escaped him."

"*Them*. Not just the demon and the Forsythes, but my stepmom and my... Goddess, Rook. My own father. I just..." She closes her eyes, blotting at fresh tears with her sleeve. "I don't understand how a father—even a terrible one—

could stand by and let his child sacrifice herself like that. Is there a chance he didn't realize what Hunter had become?"

"I wish I had an answer for you, West. At this point, we don't know your father's motivations or what he knew—or didn't know—about the demon."

"No, he knew. He *had* to know, just like Eloise. When things took a turn for the worse on that altar, I *begged* him for help. And he stared down at the floor, weak and ashamed and useless. Even if he didn't know about the fae thing, or how deep Eloise was involved in all this, he *damn* well knew it wasn't right. I was terrified, and my father did *nothing*."

I rise and join her at the fireplace, drawing her into a tight embrace. Her heart is slamming against her chest, her body quaking—with rage, with sadness, with the kind of pain only a betrayal of this magnitude can cause.

"You're *here* now, West," I whisper into her hair. "As far as we're concerned, it's his loss."

She chokes out a sob.

"I'm not trying to minimize your pain over his betrayal," I continue. "He's your dad—you're going to feel that ache for the rest of your life. But please believe me when I tell you that despite his actions—despite the actions of *everyone* in your life who disappointed or abused you—you *are* wanted and cared for. Even if it's not by your blood."

"You have no idea how much that means to me." She finally looks up at me again, a genuine smile peeking out through the tears. "Thanks."

"I'm only speaking the truth, West." I cup her face in both hands and press a kiss to her forehead, lingering for as long as I dare. When I finally pull back, a spasm between my wings has me grunting like an old man.

"Rook? What's wrong?"

"All good." I force a smile and lower myself onto the bench. "Just a little stiff. Growing pains, you know?"

"Hate to break it to you, but your setup in here is hardly ergonomic. Is your gaming lair like this, too?"

I laugh. "Worse, actually."

"You're probably working on a few decades' worth of nerve damage and spinal compression."

"Pretty sure I read about all that in a medical textbook. You'd think I'd know better."

"Most people don't learn this particular lesson until they're eating painkillers like candy and permanently strapping on the heating pad." She comes around behind me and wraps her hands around my shoulders. "May I?"

"Do you worst."

She squeezes hard enough to make me sit up *real* straight, then lightens the pressure, slowly working her way up the sides of my neck, then back down, kneading the muscles between my wings with her knuckles and thumbs.

"You're one big knot, Rook."

"At this rate? Not for long." It's taking everything in me not to moan at her expert maneuvering. "Damn, you've got strong hands for such a little witch."

"Just tell me if I'm doing it too hard."

"Not possible."

I reach for my peppermint mocha, enjoying a deep drink, enjoying everything about this moment, really. It's sheer perfection—all of it. The crackling fire, the birds fluttering around the rafters, her warm, firm touch, the soft breath stirring my hair, her eager little grunts as she works those knots out of my muscles...

Fuck.

No wonder the others can't keep their hands off her.

"You okay, professor?"

"Mmm. More than okay. Keep this up, Wild West, and you're going to put me to sleep in no time."

"Is that such a terrible thing?"

"It is when we've got a dangerous, bloodthirsty demon to assess and a stolen Codex to disarm." I sigh, the temporary perfection already fading. "I also promised Jude and Auggie I'd rig up a few more magic-dampener cuffs for their... mission."

Shit. I didn't mean to bring up the stuff about her past. But before I can apologize for sticking my big clawed foot into my big dumb mouth, she says, "It's okay, Rook. I know the guys told you about what happened to me."

I nod, no point denying it. "I was only able to track down two out of the three ringleaders so far, but don't worry. I'll get the last guy soon, and from there, we'll find every single one of the assholes involved."

"That's a lot of dampener cuffs." She laughs. "Too bad

they're mages and not fae. We could send some Midnight's Lullaby."

"Not to worry. Your man Rook has crafted the perfect cuff, unbeatable by any mage or witch for a hundred years running."

She lets out another laugh, but once again the moment —in that sneaky way of all moments—slips away.

With a deep sigh, she says, "You're working around the clock on all this research and tech stuff. Draegan's trying to keep the Archmage off our trail, not to mention fending off that asshole investigator. Jude and Auggie are gearing up to hunt down those mages..."

"And we'd do it all a thousand times over if it meant keeping you safe."

"I know. It's just... You're all risking so much for me, and I'm... I don't know. I want to help, too."

"You *are* helping. Right now, for example, you're keeping your chief researcher in top form."

"An important job, to be sure," she says, increasing the pressure on a particularly stubborn knot. "But you know what I mean. I feel like I should be more involved."

"Jude told me you're going with them tomorrow. I don't think you can get much more involved than that."

"I was planning on it, but now... I'm not so sure."

"Change of heart?"

"Draegan's worried I'll distract them and screw the whole thing up, possibly putting everyone at risk. He didn't exactly give me a chance to tell him I agree with him on this, but... yeah. He's right. If I'm there, Jude and Auggie will be more focused on keeping me safe than on getting the job done, and that's how mistakes happen. So as much as I'm dying to see the look in those bastards' eyes when Jude goes all... well, *Jude* on their asses, I think it's best if I let the guys handle it alone."

I try not to sigh in relief. "Good call."

"Besides," she says, her voice brightening, "Jude might decide to bring them back here to his workshop, and if he does? I'll volunteer to be his assistant. Win-win, right?"

"Assistant, huh? I wasn't aware he was hiring."

"He's not aware he's hiring either." She laughs, finishing up the massage with a light stroke across the tops of my wings before reclaiming her seat across from me. "Truth be told, I don't have a lot of experience being an assistant torturer—or *any* experience, really, unless you count the whole demon-stabbing thing—but I'm a quick study. Besides, I don't get squeamish around blood or severed body parts."

"Is that so?"

"Give me a hacksaw and one of those old-school hedge trimmers, throw in a pair of safety goggles, and put me to work. Fingers, toes, badly-behaved penises..." She makes a snipping motion with her fingers. "Chop-chop-chop, done and done."

"Wow. You've given this a lot of thought."

She shrugs, like *all in a day's work!*, cracking up when she catches my expression. "What? It's not like *you've* got anything to worry about, Rook. I'm sure *your* penis is *very* well-behaved."

Don't bet on it, beautiful...

"Hmm." I grin at her across the table. "You've got a twisty little kinky side I never saw coming, Wild West."

She arches an eyebrow and cocks a knowing smirk, then turns her attention back to the seminary text, highlighter poised for business. "Don't we all, professor. Don't we all."

CHAPTER SIXTEEN

WESTLYN

"Ah, these are the nights when I truly wish I'd learned more than seven languages," Draegan says wistfully. Sitting in a chair before the fireplace in the study, he flips a page of his Architectural Digest magazine and sips his drink, not bothering to look up at me. "Then I could tell you no *bloody* way in every one of them. Now for the last time, be gone. I'd like to read in peace."

"You are literally the worst." I plop down on the couch across from him. "In *every* language, worldwide. Even the extinct ones. You know that, right?"

Outside the manor's walls, the wind howls across the lawn of Blackmoor, stirring the fallen leaves into a frenzy. In here, the fire's roaring bright, the air still sweet from the hot cider and apple pie Auggie made for us earlier. Honestly, the whole catalog-worthy moment would feel downright cozy if not for the brooding gargoyle sitting here, sucking the life out of me.

Goddess. The two of us have been going at it for half an hour already, and despite busting out *all* the tricks in my arsenal, I can't get him to budge an inch.

And I need him to budge. I need him to completely *cave.* Because despite my decision not to accompany the boys on their little death squad mission tonight, I really, really, *really* need Draegan to take me to them after all.

Preferably, while the bastard mages still have some life left in them. Draegan told me he spoke to Auggie by phone earlier, confirming they nabbed Jacob Pomeroy and Alonzo Florentine without incident. Apparently, Doctor Belinda Eckhardt wasn't home, so they decided to save her "interrogation" for another night.

Thanks to a combination of gargoyle speed and strength, Rook's magic-dampener cuffs, and a couple of vials of some crazy-ass sedative, Auggie said the pair were unconscious, tied up, and tossed into the back of the Escalade before they even realized what hit them.

Draegan told me the gargoyles were in more danger from *him* for stealing one of his favorite vehicles while he was out earlier than they were from the enemy mages, but I played dumb on that particular detail.

But that phone call was over an hour ago. By now, Jake and Alonzo are likely conscious and begging for death, and who knows how much longer they'll be able to hold out, especially with Jude's fondness for blood spillage.

With a surge of renewed determination, I say, "If you don't drive me, I'll have no choice but to put on a short skirt and hitchhike to the city."

Another sigh. Another page flipped. "Sounds like an adventure. Best pack a bag—you never know where you might end up. Or who you might end up there *with*. Have you ever encountered a vampire, Miss Avery? They're particularly fond of young women in this area on account of the isolation. Fewer opportunities around here, of course, so they tend to make the most of the ones that... pop up."

Damn it.

"I know you're still pissed about our fight last night," I say, "but I'm—"

"Our fights are par for the course, love. If I held a grudge every time you mouthed off to me, I'm not sure we'd ever be on speaking terms."

Ignoring the little swoop my stomach does when the jerk calls me "love," I say, "Then what's the issue?"

No response but another page-flip.

"It's a power trip thing, right?" I press. "Nothing you love more than reminding everyone who's in charge around here." Then, in my best deep-voiced British accent, "I'm Draegan Caldwell, and I don't deviate from the schedule without a written request no less than one week in advance, because I'm the boss and I've got major control issues."

Still, nothing.

I roll my eyes to the ceiling—not that he's paying attention. "You are so *beyond* infuriating, there's not even a word for—"

"You're less protected out there," he finally says, his voice tight. "*That's* the issue. Here at Blackmoor, Rook's security system ensures nothing gets in without an invitation—not even a shadow mage. But cross that property line, and you're instantly exposed. Instantly a target for the Forsythes and every one of their mage minions, not to mention whatever demons might be involved in ensuring Zorakkov's longevity. At this point, Forsythe may have other supernaturals on his payroll as well. Vampires being top of mind. It's too risky. There are simply too many unknowns."

"But the shadow mages don't know where I am," I say. "They can't track me unless they know roughly where to look—that's the limitation of their magic. Which means whoever they've got on the payroll won't be able to find me, either."

"And what do you suppose happens the moment they get so much as a *hint* as to your whereabouts?"

"We'll just have to make sure they don't." I rise from the couch and pace before the fireplace, unwilling to give up. "Draegan, look. I'm sorry about last night. I implied you weren't holding up your end of the bargain, and that isn't true at all. I *know* you're doing what you can to protect me, and I also know it's not an easy task."

"It would be easier if you'd allow us to do our jobs without pushing back against every simple request."

"How do you see this working out? Long term, I mean. Let's say you manage to take down the Archmage, the demon prince, my father and Eloise, and everyone else connected to this whole Zorakkov thing. How will we ever know it's truly safe? The shadow magic society is huge. Worldwide. For all we know, every single mage and witch associated with it might be involved in this, from the lowest members to the most high-ranking magical officials."

"All the more reason for you to stay put."

"Forever? Is that seriously your grand plan? Keep me locked up like a princess in a tower until I die of old age or boredom?"

"If you're bored," he says, licking his index finger and turning another page, "I could put you to work cleaning out the gutters. The fall leaves are wreaking havoc on them."

A current of frustration ripples through me, but I take a deep breath and try a new tact. "I don't expect you to understand this, but I need to be there tonight. That's not me being dramatic. It's the truth."

"What happened to not wanting to distract them from the mission? Rook assured me you'd finally come to your senses about that."

"I did, but... That was before."

Flip goes another page. Pop goes the fire. Whoosh goes the wind against the walls. And then, finally, he lowers that damned magazine and meets my gaze, his own dark and stormy. "Before *what*?"

I take my seat on the couch again. "This is going to sound crazy, but—"

"I've come to expect nothing less from you."

"I'm serious. About an hour ago, I started getting this weird feeling I couldn't shake. Like something bad was coming—really bad. So I grabbed my Tarot deck, asked the cards to tell me what I most needed to know about tonight, and started shuffling. These three jumped right out of the deck and landed in my lap, all face up." I pluck the cards from my sweatshirt pocket and fan them out in my hand, holding them up for Draegan to see.

Ace of Swords, The Tower, and Death.

"It wasn't just a clumsy shuffle?" he asks.

"No way. The only time cards ever jump out at me is when they're trying really hard to tell me something. I've learned to listen."

"Okay. So what am I looking at?" He sips his drink, then leans forward for a better look. "My divination skills are a bit... nonexistent."

"The Ace of Swords came first." I hand him the card that depicts a silver sword rising from the surface of a calm lake, the blade etched in runes. "Sometimes it reminds me to seize the moment, or to be on the lookout for a new breakthrough or sudden burst of clarity about whatever's troubling me. Tonight, though, the message was kind of literal."

"Message?"

"As soon as I picked it up, I felt like I was holding a

blade. Like my hand was curled tight around the grip, and it felt heavy and solid and completely real, even though I was looking right at my hand and seeing nothing but a card."

"Does that usually happen?" he asks.

"Never—not like this. What's worse... I could feel *blood*, Draegan. Warm blood running down the blade and onto my hand. But instead of scaring the shit out of me like it should have? It made me feel powerful. This weird sense of rightness came over me. Almost like a justification for something." I shake my head, the feeling still so clear I can practically smell the coppery tang of that blood.

"Which card came next?"

"The Tower—probably the most hardcore card in the deck. It portends a major change or upheaval—we're talking sudden, brutal, and usually earth-shattering." I pass him the card, and he narrows his eyes at the image—a vicious storm attacking a massive brick building, lightning arcing down from above, setting the whole thing ablaze. Huge pieces of it have already crashed down to the street below, and you just know there won't be a single piece of it left when the storm's finally over. "This time, instead of a vision, I heard a voice in my head. Quiet, but clear as day."

"What did it say?"

"It was a verse. I've never heard anything like it before."

Holding his gaze, I whisper the chant, each word like an icy finger scraping down my spine:

Upon those screaming hours

Bathed in blood and breath
You will give them light, my moon
And I will give them Death.

On the last word, I pass him the final card—a pale skeleton dressed in black armor, riding a white mare through a field of bloodied corpses.

"Death," Draegan whispers. "I will give them Death."

"When I touched the Death card," I say, "it felt like ice running through my veins. It was so cold and terrifying, it almost took my breath away. But just when I thought my heart might literally stop, that ice-cold touch turned warm, and again I felt that sense of calm and rightness. It lasted a minute or so, and then it was gone. Everything went back to normal, like it never happened at all. I tried touching each card again, tried calling back the visions and voices, but... nothing. It was like the line went dead. The messages stayed with me, though."

Stock still in the chair across from me, staring at Death, Draegan is silent for so long I'm sure he's about five seconds from flinging the cards at me and scolding me for being such a trite and terrible witch.

Just like Eloise did when I drew the Moon card on my wedding night.

But when he finally looks up at me again, his eyes aren't mocking at all. They're serious and contemplative.

And very, *very* worried.

CHAPTER SEVENTEEN
WESTLYN

"The building in this card," Draegan says, holding up the Tower, "looks uncannily like the facility where Jude and Augustine are holding the prisoners. Right down to the number of stories, the alleyway running along the western perimeter, and the style and color of the exterior bricks."

Goosebumps ripple across my scalp and down my arms.

"Something huge is about to go down," I say, my voice soft before the crackling fire. "I'm *supposed* to be there tonight, Draegan. I've got a role to play, and if I don't show up, I just know something bad's going to happen. It's not just the Tarot cards, either. I can feel it in my gut."

"I don't doubt it, but if something bad is on the horizon, perhaps you're being warned to stay as far away from it as possible. In fact, that would be my vote, all things considered."

"Your vote shouldn't count more than mine."

Draegan lets out an exasperated sigh. "Why do you insist on throwing yourself into danger? First with the Archmage and his wife at dinner—a stunt that almost got you kidnapped. Then you practically begged me to put you in touch with Eloise, and now this? I'm sorry. I don't doubt your intuition or your divinations, but I can't in good conscience let you do this."

Passing the cards back to me, he downs the last of his drink and returns his attention to Architectural Digest.

But screw *that*. I've come too far to back down now.

Shooting to my feet and ripping the magazine out of his hands, I say, "The night those guys tied me to the tracks and basically left me for dead? That was the night I met my ravens. They saved my life, Draegan. And when I finally got out of that torture chamber, I looked up at the few stars visible in the city sky—stars I didn't think I'd ever see again—and made two promises. One, that I'd always look after my new companions—that wherever I ended up, I'd protect and help them, just like they protected and helped me. And two—"

"Wait, don't tell me. You'd paint a target on your back and march down Broadway with a bullhorn, calling out to your enemies and—"

"*Two*," I grind out. "I vowed that for as long as I still drew breath in this body, I'd *never* let anyone make me feel powerless again. And while I've taken excellent care of my birds, I'm ashamed to say I haven't been so great at keeping my second promise. The promise I made to *me*."

Draegan rubs his eyebrows and sighs again. "Miss Avery, I didn't mean—"

"The Archmage, Hunter, my own father and stepmom… They're *all* trying to make me feel powerless. They've been doing it my whole life, and you know what? I let them. You ask me why I insist on throwing myself into danger? Because sitting back and avoiding it is what got me into this mess in the first place. For nearly twenty-three years, I let everyone else call the shots and tell me what to do because I was too scared and naïve to know there was another way. I followed their orders without pushing back because I was told by all manner of adults—on a daily basis from the moment I could understand words—that I was lucky my father didn't abandon me to the wolves. That I needed to shut up and be grateful he was willing to take care of me. That I was a burden no father should've had to bear. I truly believed that my lack of magic—a thing I had absolutely zero control over—meant I didn't deserve to have a voice in my own life. I let them convince me I was completely worthless—not just as a witch, but as a human being."

"*Nothing* could be further from the truth," he says adamantly.

"You're right. And for the first time, I actually believe it, too. Here's the big secret, Draegan. The key to life. All you need is one person in your corner—just one person who's ride-or-die for you, come what may. But if you don't have that? You can be your *own* one person. Your *own* ride-or-die. That means you believe in your damn self and cheer yourself on and when shit gets really hard, you don't fucking back down. When I first fled that wedding, I was terrified of leaving my family. But I've come farther in these past few weeks with you guys than I have in the twenty-some years before, and I *refuse* to bail on myself now. Just because I'm not physically powerful like a gargoyle, or magically powerful like an Archmage, that doesn't mean I can't fight for what I believe in or stick up for myself or fucking pay attention when my gut is *screaming* at me to show up for the guys I care about, even if I don't know exactly why. So yeah, fine, you might be able to stop me this time, because I don't have a car and I'm not about to hitch a ride with bloodsuckers. Maybe you'll stop me next time, too, and the time after that. But you can't keep me locked up forever. One of these nights, I'm going to find a way to get out there and fully reclaim what I lost on the tracks that night, and you guys won't be able to protect me from that. I won't let you, because that's mine, and I fucking earned it."

By the time I get it all out, I'm panting like a dog and my heart is thundering like the storm in the Tower card and Draegan is just staring at me openmouthed, his eyes shining with something that looks a lot like wonder.

The fire pops and hisses, the air between us electrified, my whole body wired.

"Please say something," I whisper, unable to bear the intensity in his dark gray eyes.

"I can't," he says softly. "I'm still trying to decide whether you're hopelessly naïve or... extremely courageous."

"Can I be the tie-breaker and go with... extremely courageous?"

The barest hint of a smile twitches his lips, and I bounce on my toes, my stomach swirling with nerves. Goddess, I'm like a kid on Christmas, hoping against the odds she'll find a new bike under the tree instead of the usual five-dollar Starbucks gift card and pair of fuzzy socks...

"Okay, Miss Avery. If you *insist* on chasing down trouble, I suppose the least I could do is make sure you arrive there safely."

"Really? You'll take me?" I ask, my grin stretching ear-to-ear now.

But before I can kick off the celebratory dancing, Draegan holds up a finger, effectively putting my party on pause.

"But only because I'm heading into the city anyway," he says.

"Hey, I'll take it any way I can get it. Got big plans tonight? A date, perhaps?"

Beneath his dark gray skin, a hint of color stains his cheeks, there and gone in a blink. "Hardly. I've got a meeting in midtown with another investigator."

"Are they still harassing you about my so-called missing persons case?"

"Yes, but this is about another matter—the unsolved case of a murdered judge. Not our doing, but the feds have been circling us like vultures anyway."

"I'm sorry."

"Don't be." He rises from the chair and squeezes my shoulder, the briefest flicker of kindness shining in his eyes. "Right now, I just want you to focus on what's going on with those mages. Gut feelings are important, but you'll need to keep a clear head tonight, too."

"Thank you. I will. I promise." In an uncharacteristic show of appreciation for the broodiest, grumpiest gargoyle to ever brood and grump, I fling myself at him and wrap my arms around his waist, squeezing tight.

He gives me a quick, awkward pat on the head, then says, "Go get changed, then meet me in the car—we need to leave soon or I'll miss my meeting."

"Can we fly?"

"No."

"Can I drive?"

"No."

"What? Why not?"

"Aren't you a little young to have a license?" he teases.

"Aren't you a little *old* to have a license? That salt-and-pepper hair of yours is looking a little saltier these days. When was your last vision test, anyway? Elderly drivers are a danger to themselves and others."

"If that's how you feel, perhaps you should stay home tonight after all. I wouldn't want you to compromise your impeccable safety standards by getting into the car with an ancient—"

"Never mind, never mind." I flash a beatific smile. "This is my shutting-up-and-showing-respect-for-my-elders face."

"Hmm. You're *almost* cute when you do that." He rolls his eyes and turns on his heel, bringing up his human glamour, impeccably suited-and-tied, as always. "The car leaves the garage in five minutes, Miss Avery. With or without you."

CHAPTER EIGHTEEN

JUDE

"You know the best part about a hard night's work?" I take a liberal puff of my witchweed ciggy, grinning as the potent herb buzzes through my bloodstream. Fast-acting stuff, that. "Smoke breaks."

Next to me, Auggie leans back against the metal prep counter and sighs. "Personally, I could use a drink. Should've brought a flask. Mental note for next time."

"Oy! What about you lot?" I call across the cold, cement-walled space, where two naked and chained mage bastards dangle upside down from meat hooks. "Hanging in there like little champs! If anyone deserves a break tonight, it's you."

I *think* they mumble in agreement, but it's hard to discern the words amidst all their blubbering. The chains aren't cooperating either, rattling as they are with every involuntary jerk and spasm, sending all the other rusty hooks into a squeaky symphony.

Ah, but I do love the Ryker building. One of our best investments, if you ask me. The old meat processing plant doesn't have *quite* the familiar coziness of my workshop at the manor, but it's got all the original slaughterhouse machinery, including a few upgrades I made for the sake of efficiency. *So* many fun and interesting ways to keep the party going—quite literally till the break of dawn.

I laugh. Truth is, we've only been at it about half an hour. We decided to stay in our human glamours for the occasion, so it took us a bit longer to get everything set up, and then we had to wait for the sedative to wear off.

All a matter of perspective, though. I'm sure our guests feel like they've already endured a week's worth of torture.

Taking one last drag on the weed, I saunter over to the pair of most-certainly-*not* USDA-certified beef slabs and stamp out the butt in Jacob Pomeroy's belly button.

I adjust my hairnet—another treasure courtesy of the old plant—and give him a moment to process his new reality. There's a good bit of howling involved.

When he finally settles down, I peek into the trough positioned beneath them and let out a low whistle.

"That's a *lot* of blood, innit? Shame it's all going to waste." I inhale deeply, closing my eyes in appreciation. "The scent of it, though. Truly intoxicating. Am I right, Augs?"

Rejoining me to inspect our progress, Auggie sighs and says, "It's more of an acquired taste."

"Acquired taste?" I scoff. "You know, everyone likes to go on about aromatherapy candles and essential oils, but for *my* money, who needs overpriced, factory-made bullshit like *Homestead Vanilla* or *Soothing Lavender Honeysuckle* when you've got raw fear and freshly spilled blood bringing your senses to life?" I take another big breath through my nose and grin, shimmying my shoulders. "Oooh, it's downright *tingly*."

Auggie rolls his eyes and leans in with his camera, trying to get a good angle for his next series of shots.

When it comes to my work, I don't normally allow photography—some things are best left undocumented, naturally—but I made an exception tonight. Bloodlust is unpredictable; I might miss a few clues in the heat of the frenzy.

With Auggie's talent for lighting and keen eye for detail, he can capture the moments as they unfold, giving us all an opportunity to peruse the evidence later.

Like many things when it comes to our witch, *this* requires a team effort.

The flash pops a few times. Our guests wince at the bright light.

"What about you, Jakey?" I ask dangling corpse number one. "You feeling any tingles?"

Gasping and pale, he sputters, "I... I can't feel my... my toes."

I glance at Auggie and shake my head. "Mages these days, Augs, I tell you. *Zero* critical thinking skills."

"Why can't I feel my t-t-toes?" he tries again, crocodile tears plopping into the blood trough below.

I crouch down in front of him so we're eye level, bringing my mouth close to the ear I mangled when I first strung him up tonight.

"Because," I whisper. Then, gripping his hair, I shout, "I chopped them off with a fucking meat cleaver, you twat!"

Rising up to my full height again, I punch him in the gut —punishment for being so bloody stupid. Knocks the wind right out of him, too.

He swings on the meat hook. Poor Auggie has to jump out of the way to avoid a direct hit.

"And you, Zo-Zo?" I move on to dangling corpse number two, Alonzo Florentine. "You feeling any of those tingles?"

"F-f-fuck you," he stammers, finally offering a few words, which is a rather nice surprise. All we got during the warm-up was snot and tears. "You're a d-d-dead man."

"Oh, I can see that. Clearly." I cradle his head in both hands, wrenching it up so I can look down into his eyes.

I try to imagine what he looked like a decade ago, before the facial hair and the defined jaw.

I try to imagine what he looked like as a young student mage, bright-eyed and eager to learn.

I try to imagine what he looked like on the night he assaulted my little scarecrow.

Earlier, when our guests first regained consciousness, I

asked them about her. Repeated her name several times, demanded to know what it meant to them.

I was so calm and un-Jude-like, Auggie said I deserved an award. Couldn't believe I didn't eviscerate them and hang them from their own intestines rather than messing with the chains.

Don't get me wrong—nothing would've brought me more joy.

But they would've died too quickly. Too easily.

Through all the questions, both mages played dumb. Claimed they didn't remember a classmate by that name. Insisted, despite Rook's video evidence, they weren't at the Forsythe wedding last month. They barely even knew the Archmage, they said.

When I asked for the name of the young girl they brutalized ten years ago in an abandoned subway station—if not Westlyn Avery, then who?—they said it never happened. Swore on their mothers' lives it was just an urban legend, some bullshit story about a vengeful witch who haunts the old station and chases kids through the tunnels, sacrificing her prey to the demons.

That was the part of the show when poor Jakey lost his toes. I told him I was rooting for the vengeful witch, and I wanted to give her a better shot at catching him.

By the way, if you've never seen a man piss himself while he's dangling upside down? That alone is worth the price of admission. Put it on your bucket list, mate.

"You're not a bad-looking bloke, Zo-Zo," I say now.

"Nice, thick mane. Good bone structure. Shame about the speech impediment, though."

He tries to jerk out of my grasp. "Wh-what? I don't have a—"

"You claim you don't know Westlyn Avery, but she sure knows you. In fact, you know what she told me?" I stroke his hair, my touch as soft and gentle as my voice. "She said you were her first kiss. Did you know that?"

"She's... she's lying. That little s-s-slut is—"

"Have you ever been kissed against your will, Zo-Zo?" I ask, his insults beginning to crack my calm demeanor. "Ever had something stolen from you? A rare and precious thing you could *never* get back?"

"F-fuck off, you sick fuck. I'm gonna enjoy—"

"Enjoy what?" I crush his jaw in a vise grip, forcing his mouth open. "This? I very much doubt it, but hey, I'm no kink-shamer."

Then, while he's wriggling and gagging, wriggling and gagging, I give him a big ol' smackeroo on the mouth, bite down hard on his tongue, and tear it *right* the fuck out.

CHAPTER NINETEEN

JUDE

Alonzo does not, in fact, enjoy it.

Blood spills over my chin and down into his nose and eyes, and I shove him away, sending him swinging on the hook, more blood painting the cement.

Now Jake's on a crying jag again, too. Honestly, I can't decide which of them is the bigger fucking baby—tie score at the moment.

I jerk the bloody tongue out of my mouth, then stuff it firmly into Jake's, temporarily silencing him. "Spit that out before I say so, and I'll cut off your dick and feed it to the rats." By the time I turn my attention back to Alonzo, I'm feeling much better, all cool and collected and professional again. "Now. About that speech impediment... Anything to share with the class, Zo-Zo?"

His eyes are wild and bloody, his cries of agony echoing

across the perpetually damp walls. Pretty sure he's trying to say something insightful, but...

"Sorry, mate. Can't understand a *bloody lick* of that." I laugh and wriggle my eyebrows. "Get it? A bloody lick?"

No response but the tears.

"Seriously? Not even a smile? From either of you?" I shake my head. "Damn, it's like someone tore out your senses of humor, too."

"*Jude.*" Auggie glares at me, exhaustion creasing his human face, taking a bit of the shine out of his normally oh-so-lustrous hair. "Maybe we could speed things along? I'd *really* like to skip ahead to the part where I'm *not* wading through blood and body parts while being forced to endure your stand-up routine, as entertaining as you are." He flashes a bored smile.

"Everyone's a critic," I sigh. "Very well.." I swap out my soiled hairnet for a clean one, then select the meat cleaver from the array of tools on the counter behind us, feeling rather official about the whole thing.

"So, Jakey." I remove Alonzo's tongue from his mouth and toss it into the trough. "Since you've still got *your* tongue, tell me about your man, Full Metal Jacket."

Through a bloody sputter, he grunts, "Who?"

"Are you pulling my leg?" I laugh and shake a finger at him, like, *you got me!* "So you *do* have a sense of humor! I'm glad. In these trying times, nothing's more important. Laughter *is* the best medicine, after all, and you're going to need some *good* healing after this night." I spin him around on the chains so I can reach his hands, then lob off the tip of a middle finger. Eh, maybe it's two fingers. Hard to be precise with such a big blade and all those teeny, tiny digits.

More screaming, of course.

Bo-ring.

"Another mental note for the list, Augs," I say, wincing. "Stock the facility with earplugs." Then, raising my voice above Jake's incessant whining, "Time to focus, Jake. Deep breaths. Full Metal Jacket, right? Don't hold back. I want *all* the salacious details."

Auggie snaps a few more pictures for the family album.

"I don't... don't know anyone called Full Metal J-Jacket. I swear." Jake blinks against the harsh light of the flash. He's full-on panting now, covered in sweat and blood and piss, face as pale as paper.

Fairing better than Zo-Zo, though. That motherfucker is passed out cold again, blood drooling out of his slack mouth.

I hate when they conk out early.

No matter. We'll be sure to wake him up in time for the grand finale.

"You sure about that?" I ask Jake.

"I swear. I... I never heard of him."

"Hmm. My mistake, then." I nod to Auggie, and he smashes a big red button on the wall with his fist.

Ancient, rusty gears grind to life, and with the hellacious screech of metal on metal, all the meat hooks start moving down the line, chains clanking as they go. With slow, steady steps, I accompany our guests on the fifty-foot journey to their new destination:

Hovering just above the industrial-strength meat grinder.

"That's good, Auggie," I call out.

Auggie hits the stop button.

And I hit the power switch on the grinder.

The thing's about as loud as an old steamer train, and just as rickety, but all the parts are still in good working order—that was the first thing I checked when we arrived tonight.

I make sure to point this out to Jake, who—in a shocking twist of events—starts balling again.

I'm about to signal to Auggie to lower the hooks when the bastard finally cures himself of his amnesia.

"Conrad Nesterman!" he shouts, clearer than he's been all night. "That's Metal's name. Lives out in Bayside with his girlfriend now. A witch named K-K-Kelly Obrovski."

I put the grinder on standby. "Keep talking."

"That's it. You wanted a name, you got it."

"I'm still waiting on a confession, Jake. Westlyn Avery, remember? Girl you used to call Wicked?"

Just saying the word sends a poison ache through my gut, the image of her scars flashing behind my eyes. Her tears. Her shame.

"I told you," he says. "That's just an urban—"

"Going with the legend bit again? Wow. And here I thought we were building something special together,

Jakey." I turn the grinder on high speed and signal to Auggie, who lowers the hooks until Jake's head is a mere foot from achieving its destiny.

"Wait!" He screams, his whole body trembling. "Wait! You were right. It wasn't a s-story. It was us. The g-g-girl on the tracks... We got paid five grand a p-p-piece to—"

"Five *grand?*" I silence the grinder again. "Each?"

"Yeah," he says, and I swear the arsehole's lips twitch like he's about to smile. Like I might actually be impressed with his ability to command such a high price.

Well. That is *definitely* the wrong move here.

Fucking hell, I'm vibrating with the rage of it all, the blood sizzling in my veins. The only reason—and I do mean the *only* reason—these twin fuckstains aren't a pile of chunky soup in a bucket right now is because they might still have some useful intel.

I close my eyes. Take a deep breath. Count backward from ten and bask in the aromatic scents of fear and blood.

Delayed gratification, I remind myself. *Old school, legendary patience, just how I like it...*

"Five grand," I repeat softly. "Five grand was the fair market price for brutalizing and assaulting a young girl, leaving her with permanent scars, and traumatizing her for the rest of her—oh, wait! That's right. You didn't think she'd *have* the rest of her life. You left her for dead on the tracks."

He's not smiling anymore, that's for sure. "No. No! That

was an accident. We weren't supposed to k-k-kill her. They wanted her alive—just scared. Primed, they said."

"Primed? What the fuck does that even mean? Who paid you? Why did they want her scared? How many were involved? For fuck's sake, Pomeroy, who were you working for?"

It's a lot of questions to throw at him, but I'll take any answer, player's choice.

Unfortunately, the player doesn't respond. Just keeps trembling. Sniffling. Pretty sure he's on his way out.

"Auggie!" I call. "Bring me that metal bin, would you, love?"

A moment later, Auggie joins us and hands it over—current home of Jake's toes.

I turn on the grinder again.

"Who," I say, calmly plucking a big toe from the bin and tossing it into the grinder. "Paid." Baby toe, this time. "You?" I dump in the rest in one go, Jake looking on with fresh horror, arching his back in a failed attempt to get away from the red mist.

When he finally confesses, it's barely a whisper.

I turn off the machine. It belches black smoke into the air. Jake coughs and spits up blood.

"Say that name again," I demand, certain I misunderstood, but knowing—just fucking *knowing*—I didn't.

"Eloise," he pants. "Eloise DeFoe."

Westlyn's fucking stepmother. That was her name before she married Brian Avery. And ten years ago? Fuck, she wasn't even part of the family yet, which means she was plotting against Westlyn even before she allegedly met her father.

And if she was already involved in this shitshow a decade ago, chances are she was involved more than *two* decades ago, too, when Westlyn was born and Hunter started those treatments—both at the very hospital where Eloise worked in pediatrics.

I exchange a glance with Auggie. I can tell by the dark look in his eyes, he's just made the same damn calculations.

"What did Eloise want with the girl?" Auggie asks Jake, the deep, familiar sound of his voice the only thing keeping me sane right now, because I swear to the fucking *devil*, if he wasn't here asking the questions, Jake's head would already be hamburger.

"She wanted us to b-break her," Jake says. "To make sure the witch was d-d-docile."

"Why?" he asks.

"She didn't tell us at the time. But I'm g-guessing it was all for the... the demon ceremony."

"What do you know about the arranged marriage between Westlyn Avery and Hunter Forsythe?" I ask. "Why her, and not some other witch?"

"I don't know, man!" he screeches. "I don't fucking know! I'm not some high-ranking mage. Just... Fuck! I've told you everything... P-P-Please!"

I grab his throat and squeeze until his eyes bulge, my fingers slippery with his blood. "Why the *fuck* did they spend all that time torturing a young girl just so they could pawn her off to a fucking *demon*? Why did Lennon Forsythe conspire with Brian—"

"Jude. *Enough*." Auggie's firm command snaps me out of it, and I release Jake's throat, taking a step back and trying to get my bearings again. I'm shaking, my heart booming in my chest, my vision red with blood and fury both.

"Pretty sure we got all we're gonna get from them," Auggie says.

I mutter a curse, but he's right. I've been in the business long enough to know when someone's "I don't know" is a lie or a bid to cover their arse.

But this time? It means the bastard truly doesn't fucking know.

"Thank you, gentlemen. Good work." Blowing out a breath, I glance at Auggie and nod, letting him know I'm okay. "I believe we're done with the interrogation, then?"

"All set," he confirms.

Jake brightens. "Can... can we go?"

"Yeah, sure," I say with a casual shrug. "Why not?"

"Wait... Really?"

Ah, that shimmering hope. Such a lovely thing to give that gift, only to snatch it right back again.

"Not on your fucking life," I growl, "which isn't worth much more than your liquified toes, so that's not a bet *I'm* taking. Auggie? You want to play guarantor to this pair of worthless twats?"

Auggie laughs—a real one this time. "I'm no wolf of Wall Street, Jude, but even *I* know that's a shit investment."

"Sorry, Jake. Better luck never." I glance around the facility, trying to determine our next play now that the interrogation bit is over. But first... "I need another smoke. Augs, do me a favor and see if you can find one of the old cattle prods. A few volts up the arse oughta rouse sleeping beauty here—don't want Zo-Zo to miss out on the fun."

Auggie returns a few minutes later with not one, but two prods.

I grin, cigarette dangling from my lips. "Well, aren't you just a regular Santy-Clause."

"Merry fucking Christmas, brother."

I'm just about to give the old thing a whirl when my phone buzzes—text from Draegan.

Bringing Westlyn to you—she insisted. Meet me on the parking level in 10.

I text back immediately. *On my way.*

Heading over to the old sinks along the wall behind the counter, I dunk my head under the faucet and give myself a good dousing—can't very well kiss my girl when I've got another man's blood in my mouth.

"What are you smiling about now?" Auggie asks the moment I come up for air.

"Apparently, I've been a *very* good boy this year, because the gifts just keep on coming." I shove my wet hair back off my face and wink. "Looks like the little scarecrow will be joining us for the final festivities, after all."

CHAPTER TWENTY

WESTLYN

So much for a clear head.

I meant to keep my promise to Draegan about that. Really, I did.

We made the entire drive down here in relative peace with minimal bickering, and for a while, we even managed to achieve the elusive "comfortable silence" status of almost, sorta kinda, actual... friends.

But the moment he slows the car and the old Ryker Meat Packing Plant comes into view, every hair on my arms stands on end, and a strange, cold tingle slithers down my spine, sinking into my gut like a block of ice.

He was right earlier. The building looks a lot like the one in The Tower card.

Now, as he turns down a concrete ramp and heads into the facility's dark, decrepit underground parking garage, the unsettling vibes only intensify.

Something feels terribly *wrong* here... which only confirms I'm in *exactly* the right place.

Draegan puts the car in park. For a long beat, he stares out the windshield, the muscle on his jaw flexing. Finally, he turns to look at me, pinning me with his steely, unwavering gaze. He kept up the glamour for the drive down, but those storm-cloud eyes never change. "You're certain you want to do this?"

Another wave of icy darkness washes through me, and I clench my teeth to keep them from chattering. Every instinct is shouting at me to abandon ship, but I can't, because those same instincts are being overridden by another feeling—a strange, otherworldly pull.

Fear not, little one. You belong here. Everything is unfolding as it should be...

The words drift through my mind—not a voice, not a visual, just... a certainty.

"It's not too late to change your mind," Draegan says, and I realize I've been silent for too long.

I shake my head and straighten my spine. Despite my warring instincts, I refuse to show him even an ounce of trepidation. If he sensed me wavering, he'd hit the child locks and zoom us out of here before I could even say *hot waffles*.

"I didn't come all this way to back out now," I say.

He opens his mouth to respond, but then just shakes his head and turns off the car.

With one hand protectively on my lower back, his eyes

scanning every inch of the shadowy garage for trouble, Draegan walks me to the facility's underground entrance—a set of massive metal doors that look more like something from a military installation than an abandoned factory in the Meat Packing District. Jude's already waiting for us there, and the moment he sees me, he stamps out his cigarette, a smile stretching across his human-glamoured lips.

"Hello, darling." He pulls me into a tight embrace and lifts me off my feet, burying his face against my neck. Cold water drips from his hair onto my skin. "What an unexpected surprise. Miss me already?"

"Jude." I breathe in his candles-and-black-pepper scent, holding back another shiver. "*Please* tell me they're still alive."

The request tumbles out of my mouth unbidden, barely even a conscious thought on my part. If Jude finds it odd, he doesn't show it.

"Ehh... Define *alive*."

"Do they have pulses?"

"Yes." He sets me back on my feet and shrugs. "Not for too much longer, though, so if you've got some parting words for the sodding fools, we best get moving."

A sharp, red-hot thrill shoots through my chest. After ten years of running from those mage pricks in my nightmares, I'm finally getting the chance to say all the things I *couldn't* say when I was a terrified little girl and they held all the power.

And it's all thanks to my gargoyles.

The warnings I felt earlier fade away, that feeling of utter rightness taking center stage. I don't know why I *ever* tried to talk Jude and Auggie out of hunting them down.

You belong here. Everything is unfolding as it should be...

"Let's go," I say firmly. "I'm ready."

"Yes, ma'am." Jude reaches for the door handle, but Draegan stops him with a firm grip on his shoulder.

"Do *not* let her out of your sight," Draegan says. "Any sign of distress, you get her the *fuck* out of there, no questions, no arguments."

"She'll be fine," Jude says, at the same time I say, "I'll be fine."

Draegan glowers at both of us like he's about to blow a dad-gasket, but then, glancing at his phone, he sighs and says, "I need to get back to midtown—Inspector Barrington is expecting me in half an hour. Text me when I can come retrieve her. And Jude?"

Jude holds up a finger. "You don't have to say it."

They glare at each other for an eternity, having an entire conversation without words.

Then Draegan closes his eyes, curses under his breath, and does the craziest, most unexpected thing of all.

He leans down and kisses my cheek.

He's gone without another word.

Jude leads me through a series of institutional looking hallways illuminated by a single row of harsh, bare bulbs in the ceiling. "Thought for sure you'd be holed up in the library having a nerd-off with Rook and your birds tonight, scarecrow. What changed your mind?"

"My Tarot cards."

"Really?"

I give him the quick highlights-reel version of the reading, including the part about the factory looking a hell of a lot like the Tower. "I know I sound like Batty McCrazy-Pants, but… I just know I'm supposed to be here—to see them one last time before you end things."

"Darling. The day you sound crazy to a bloke like *me* is the day you've *really* got to worry." Jude stops at another set of massive doors at the end of the last hallway. Looking me over head to toe, he says, "I hope you're not too attached to this outfit, scarecrow. Judging from that determined look in your eyes, I'd say things are about to get messy."

Again, that red-hot spark zings through me. Pulling my hair into a quick, out-of-the-way bun, I grin at him and say the only appropriate word for the occasion. "*Excellent.*"

And then, rather than talk me out of it or list all the reasons why this is a terrible idea, he pushes open the doors and says, "Let's see how long it takes you to make them shit their non-existent pants."

Standing in the middle of a concrete slaughterhouse, the scent of blood and urine heavy in the air, I stare at the two broken mages slumped against a wide cement pillar. Their hands are bound behind their backs, bodies so badly beaten I can hardly tell them apart. One is missing his toes. The other his tongue. Both are barely alive.

"They've been chained up and hanging from meat hooks most of the night," Jude says, "but Auggie has taken the liberty of putting them on the ground for you."

"*Beneath* you, as they should be." Auggie leans in to kiss my cheek. Then, in a whisper just for me, "The minute you want out, just say so. Jude and I will finish up."

"Deal," I say.

"You good?" Jude asks, and I nod, shrugging out of my jacket. Jude takes it from me, and the two gargoyles take a step back and lean against a long metal counter, giving me a little space.

I walk a slow circle around the pillar, looking over every bare inch of our captives. There's no need to guess what tortures Jude and Auggie have inflicted—the story is written in every bruise, every gouge, every electrical burn on their skin.

The pair are silent but for their labored breathing.

They watch me, tracking my every move. Their eyes are begging me for something I refuse to give them.

I take my time, making a few passes. Waiting to feel something.

Fury. Fear. Even pity.

But nothing comes.

"Do you know who I am?" I finally ask, my voice as cold as the damp cement walls.

Both mages nod.

"Do you remember what you did to me?"

This question doesn't get a response.

I unzip my hoodie and toss it to Jude.

Standing before the mages in nothing but yoga pants and a sports bra, I turn and give them my back.

My eyes are locked on my gargoyles' fierce gazes, but when I speak again, I'm talking to the monsters on the ground behind me.

"Look," I say. "Look at what you did to me. Look at every letter, every fucking scar, and remember how I *begged* you to stop." I'm still numb inside, the calm before a storm, and my voice is strong and clear. Unwavering. "Look at me and remember how you laughed at me. How you held me down and tortured me. How you pissed on me and spit in my face and left me on the tracks to fucking *die*."

A tear slips down Auggie's cheek, fists clenching at his sides. A deep, low growl hums through Jude's chest, but I shake my head, silently urging them both to stand down.

I've got this. I've fucking *got* this.

I turn to face the mages again, both still staring at me with terrified, pleading gazes.

"Do you remember now?" I ask.

Alonzo manages a small grunt. Blood leaks from his mouth.

But Jake? Jake actually grins.

"Wicked... wicked little *whore*," he breathes.

He's trembling and close to death, bruises blooming all over his face, but still. The piece of shit finds the strength to mock me, one last time.

In that moment, the strange force keeping my emotions at bay finally shatters, and everything inside me boils over like one of my infamous exploding cauldrons from Mrs. Larkum's class.

Fury. Hot and wild and unstoppable. It churns through my veins, my gut, desperate to consume.

I stalk over to the counter. The guys step aside, and I scan the array of tools spread out there—cleavers and knives, mallets, rusty pipes. A box of old hairnets that would make the proverbial lunch ladies proud.

And there, at the very end—a curved dagger, the blade gleaming.

Hello, beautiful...

The moment my fingers wrap around the handle, the rage inside me crystallizes into a sense of purpose and inner knowing so clear and precise, there's no doubt in my mind.

This is the moment the Ace of Swords predicted.

This is why I came.

This is what I must do.

You belong here. Everything is unfolding as it should be...

I return to the mages. Kneel before them.

Smile.

Everything I meant to say—everything I thought would come to me in the face of my tormentors— vanishes.

When the words finally come, I don't even recognize them as mine.

"Your last moments on earth will be filled with an agony far greater than what you caused me." I touch the tip of the blade to a pale throat. Jake's. He's no longer grinning. Piss pools on the cement beneath him. "But that agony is *nothing* compared to what you'll suffer at *his* hands."

I press the blade in the tiniest bit. A crimson drop beads on the metal.

You belong here. Everything is unfolding as it should be...

A burst of silver-white light explodes around us, and everything goes black.

CHAPTER TWENTY-ONE

AUGUSTINE

If I needed any more evidence that our mysterious fae entity is connected to West and not some disembodied spirit wandering the manor, I've got it.

The moment she picks up that blade, I feel it—that cold, hollow wind. The sickness gripping my stomach. The wave of nausea is so strong, it's all I can do not to fall to my knees and puke.

I don't, though. I force myself to remain steady, to take deep breaths through my mouth, to keep my eyes locked on the scene unfolding before us.

West is no longer with us. It's like the witch we know has checked out, the dark entity inside taking over. Her skin glows with silvery light, her eyes wide and unblinking. Aside from the athame at her wedding, she's never wielded a blade before. Yet now, she cuts with swift, precise movements, carving up every visible inch of skin she can find—a slash under Jake's arm, another on the side of his neck. Alonzo's inner thighs. The bottom of his feet. Foreheads and cheeks, shoulders and shins and knuckles.

She's not gentle. She's not merciful.

She's fucking *possessed*.

And through it all—through every slash of that blade, every upwelling of blood that follows—the mages cry out in ways so terrible, so horrifying, I've only ever heard those sounds on the battlefields of men at war.

When I finally tear my eyes away from Westlyn and meet Jude's awed gaze, a shared understanding passes between us.

Whatever this is, whatever happens, we need to let her finish it.

I don't know how much time passes, Jude and I watching the vicious dance of blade and blood and cold ethereal light.

Some instinctive part of me eventually remembers we need to document this—for Rook, for Draegan, for Westlyn herself if we've got any chance of figuring this out later—and I finally lift my camera again. I'm not even looking through the lens, though—just pointing it in the general direction of the carnage and holding down the shutter button, burning through an entire roll of film in a blink.

Then, when it feels like the moon must've set and risen five times over and there's not a single bloodless inch of skin remaining on the mages, Westlyn returns to us, pale and unsteady, the dagger trembling in her grip.

The mages behind her choke and gasp, barely clinging to the last vestiges of life, no longer able to form words.

"Witchling?" I whisper. "West?"

The light enveloping her finally dims, then vanishes, but that cold hollow feeling inside me does not.

Blood streaks her face, and when she finally meets my gaze, her eyes are ancient and haunted. In a voice that's not altogether of this world, she says, "The evil ones still draw breath."

"Not for long," I assure her, because I'm not sure what the fuck else to do but try like hell to keep her calm and remind her that everything's going to be okay, even though we're so far *beyond* the realm of okay, I'm half convinced—half *hoping*—we're all just trapped in some elaborate, temporary nightmare.

"They mustn't walk out of here alive," she says.

"They won't be walking," Jude replies, his voice soft. "They won't be alive. That's two promises for the price of one."

That same silvery light that pulsed from her skin before now gleams in her eyes, and she lifts the dagger to her mouth, licking the blood from the blade. Then, with a cruel, malicious grin, "Let us *end* it, then."

Jude casts me a dark look, the fear in his eyes nearly unraveling me.

In all our years together, I've known Jude Hendrix to be a lot of things.

Unhinged. Psychotic. Obsessive. Violent. A total asshole

and the most loyal fucking friend and brother anyone could ask for.

But I've never known him to be terrified. Not like this.

I close my eyes. Suck in a deep, steadying breath.

Keep it together, asshole. She needs you...

"Give me the blade, darling," Jude says, and I open my eyes to see her finally relinquishing it.

The moment it's out of her hand and back on the counter, that same light flashes in her eyes again, ancient and deadly, and for one horrifying heartbeat, I'm certain she's going to kill us where we stand.

But then a scream of pure agony tears through her throat, and she clutches her head, her legs finally giving out.

I catch her before she falls, scooping her up and drawing her close.

"Westlyn," I say. "West!"

We bring her to the sinks. Jude splashes cold water on her face, then fills a cupped hand and tips some of it into her mouth.

"That's it, darling," he whispers as she drinks. "Come back to us now. We're here. Just come back."

After what feels like a fucking *eon*, she finally stirs, a soft moan escaping her lips as she slowly blinks back to consciousness.

I tighten my grip on her, and Jude and I hold our breaths, waiting, fucking *hoping*...

"Auggie?" she whispers. The haze dissipates from her eyes, her brow furrowing. "What... what happened?"

Jesus fuck.

The sound of her true voice, the warmth in her blue-green eyes... It's her. In a flash, that cold wind vanishes, taking the last of my nausea with it. I close my eyes and press my lips to the top of her head, heart thudding in my chest. I can't talk around the knot of emotion lodged in my throat.

"Where... where are the mages?" she asks.

"Right where we left them." Jude thumbs toward the area on the other side of the counter, where the two assholes are still slumped against the pillar, heads lolling.

"Did I... Are they dead?" she asks.

"Almost." Jude strokes her hair. "You sliced-and-diced them pretty good. I'll finish up the rest."

"I... what?" Her brow knits with confusion. "I don't... I don't remember it. Why don't I remember it?"

I set her on her feet, taking her hands in mine and forcing a smile. "Shock response. Totally normal."

I have no idea if that's true, but right now, it seems like the only logical explanation. And I need to believe there *is* a logical explanation for this, because the alternative is too fucking horrifying to consider.

"I need to finish it." She pulls out of my hold and heads for the counter. "They need to die. Now."

"I'll take care of it," Jude says, following her.

How the fuck he can be so calm right now is beyond me. It's beyond *him*, this sudden newfound ability to keep a cool head whenever West seems to need him the most.

She grabs the dagger again, but he's right beside her, gently prying it out of her fingers.

"Give it to me," she whispers. "I need it."

With his free hand, he cups her cheek. "No, scarecrow. You've done what you came here to do. It's over now."

"Jude, I... Please. I need to kill them."

"I can't let you do that." He frowns, tracing his thumb along her lower lip. "Killing them... It'll destroy a part of you I'm not willing to give up on just yet, even if you are."

"Auggie?" She turns to look at me as I join them at the counter, her eyes pleading, tears spilling down her cheeks.

"Jude's right, witchling. This isn't something you need to do. Let him take care of it. Please?"

She glances at the mages again, then at her hands, still trembling.

She's silent for so long I worry we're losing her again, but then she finally nods, a deep, shuddering breath rattling through her.

I fold her into my embrace. Hot tears soak through my shirt.

"I don't remember it," she breathes. "I don't remember anything after picking up that knife the first time. Just... a bright light and... and then I was in your arms."

I meet Jude's gaze over the top of her head, mouthing for him to text Draegan. He needs to get here *now*. Get her the fuck out of here so Jude and I can finish the job, throw the evidence into the incinerator, and put this whole fucking night behind us.

"It's okay, witchling," I murmur, stroking her back while Jude exchanges a volley of texts with Drae. "Whatever it is, you don't have to worry about it now. We'll figure it out at home. Let's just clean up a bit, okay?"

She allows me to bring her back to the sinks, where I help her wash the blood from her hands and face. There's still a bit smudged around her hairline, but at least she looks more like herself again and less like... Well, less like fucking Jude.

"Better?" I ask.

"I... I'm not..." She blows out another shuddering breath and looks up at me again, her eyes wide and lost and glazed with some new, inexplicable fright. "Um... Auggie?"

"Hey. Hey, take a breath. You're okay. You're just—"

"Something's wrong with me. All of a sudden, I feel..." She closes her eyes and swallows hard, her heartbeat ratcheting up a few notches.

Fuck. Even with the human glamour dimming my gargoyle senses, I can still hear it thudding away inside her —just like I can scent the sudden, inexplicable spike of her desire.

She clutches my arms and looks up at me again, her breathing ragged. "I... I need you to touch me. I'm burning up and... I can't... I feel so... *hungry*."

Hungry...

The hot, breathy way she says that word...

No, she's definitely not talking about my apple muffins and vegan waffles, as award-winning as they are.

"Auggie?" She slides her palms up my chest, her touch hot and trembling, her gaze searching my face, the look in her eyes wild and desperate and a little bit baffled, as if she truly can't understand what's come over her.

When she speaks again, her voice is a harsh whisper, her cheeks dark with lust.

"Please. I just... Don't judge me, but I... I need you to make me come. *Now*."

CHAPTER TWENTY-TWO

AUGUSTINE

Well, damn.

I don't know where the fuck this is coming from. I don't know what the fuck's going on inside her head. I don't know the fucking deal with that unformed dark entity I felt, or the otherworldly light I saw, or Westlyn's sudden onset memory loss pertaining to the mages she sliced up.

But I do know this:

There's no fucking *way* I'm going to allow a woman I care about—*this* fucking woman—to suffer needlessly. Not when it's in my power to fix it and the solution is so damned easy. Touching her? Making her come for me? Yeah. In a night of a thousand fucked-up wrong turns and miscalculations, *this* is a thing I can actually accomplish.

With. Fucking. Pleasure.

Maybe it's sick and twisted, maybe we've both got terrible timing, maybe the devils we meet at the end of days will shake their heads and cast us out of hell for such an indiscretion, but when my little witch looks at me like she's looking at me right now, her chest rising and falling, her lush lips parted...

It's hard to care about anything else in the world but giving her *exactly* what she needs.

So, shoving aside all my worries and unanswered questions, I flash her a sly grin, hooking my fingers into the waistband of her pants and drawing her close. "I've got you, witchling. I've fucking got you."

Dipping my head low, I run my nose down the slope of hers, then claim her in a searing-hot kiss, groaning into her mouth as she parts for me, her soft little tongue darting out to taste mine, her breath sweet and hot, my cock pressing hard against my pants...

"Wait!" she gasps. All too soon, she's breaking away from me, panting and shaking her head. "Not... not like this. I need the real you."

"I'm right here, witchling. It's me. It's always been me."

"No. I'm talking about *you*, Augustine Lamont. Not the glamour you wear to fool everyone else. But the gargoyle I..." She stretches up on her toes and presses her palm to my cheek, a moment of sweetness in the midst of our dark depravity. "The gargoyle who bought me real maple syrup and let me touch his wings and kisses me like he might starve if he has to go a whole night without it."

Something inside my heart—some wild, needy thing I thought I locked up and forgot about long ago—cracks open at her words. At her smile. At the light in her eyes—the real light. The light that's *all* Westlyn Avery.

Warmth floods my chest, exhilarating and terrifying and a complete fucking wonder to me now. If I've ever felt this way about another person before, I sure as hell don't remember it.

Not like this.

We've never talked about it—the fact that West could have us either way. Men, monsters, even a bit of both—a quick-change artist between the sheets, guaranteed to satisfy every craving from the stuff so vanilla you could *almost* do it in church, to the sort of triple-X, five-alarm fantasies that are illegal in at least half the states and usually best left to the professionals.

Our glamours are more than just visual. As long as we've got them in place, to any outsider who looks at us, touches us, fucks us... We're as real as any human man on the street. Or, in the case of supernaturals, as real as any fae male.

West never asked if it was possible. Never seemed to look at us as anything other than who we were. From the moment we revealed our true selves, she accepted us, no question.

Before tonight, I only ever kissed her as a gargoyle. Touched her as a gargoyle. Felt her lush lips around my gargoyle cock, brought her into my gargoyle bed, and made love to her with my gargoyle tail and claws and tongue and every monstrous part of me.

Even when I shared her with Jude, it was only ever as a gargoyle.

As me.

If I wasn't already falling for her... Yeah. Pretty sure this would fucking do it.

I glance over at Jude, who's just slipping his phone back into his pocket. He gives me a nod—Draegan must be on his way—then grabs the dagger from the countertop, returning his attention to the mages.

They'll be gone soon enough. No need to keep up appearances.

I drop the human mask and let the gargoyle loose, a desperate ache pulsing through my balls as the full intensity of West's desire crashes into my heightened senses.

Jude senses it, too. He glances at us over his shoulder, his eyes darkening with lust, even as the mages manage one last gasp of fresh horror at this new revelation—a dark, dangerous, winged beast, with fangs and claws and an insatiable appetite for destruction.

But West? The way she's looking at me now... *Fuck*. A mischievous smile curves her lips, her gaze absolutely *feral* with need.

All I want to do is bend her over the counter, tear off those pants, and *bury* myself deep inside her, forgetting everything but the feel of her soft skin, her heat...

But... no. This isn't the time or the place. Not for me.

Right now, West needs this more than I do. Some hot,

filthy pleasure to bring her right back to her body. To the moment. To the gargoyles who've sworn to protect her.

A growl tears through my chest. Hovering close to her mouth again, I whisper darkly, "Turn around, witchling. Pull down your pants and put your hands on the counter."

She obeys me at once, the clothing pooling around her ankles.

"Bend over and let me see that tight, beautiful ass," I command, and she does. "Now close your eyes for me."

Seems I've finally found her hard limit, because after all that, suddenly she's shaking her head.

"I can't," she whispers. "I need to see him, Auggie. Please. I need to see him end it."

Jude hears it. Glances over at us again. His gaze locks onto hers, fierce and determined. Then he shifts those crazy blue eyes to me, his intention clear.

His glamour falls away in an instant, revealing the massive gargoyle inside.

He moves to the side of the pillar, giving West and me a clear view of the quivering, sputtering mages.

Damn.

This is some dark shit, even for us.

But I can't say no to her on this one, and neither can Jude.

And I'm not gonna lie... this is... *fuck*. I'm not sure what the fuck it says about me, but here it is:

I've never been so fucking turned on in my life.

I run my palm up her spine and fist her hair, tugging it

loose from the bun and wrapping it around my clawed fist, pulling it until she tips her head back.

"Watch him," I growl. "Watch your gargoyle slit their throats while your other gargoyle makes you come all over his tail."

"Goddess, yes," she breathes, and that's all the invitation we need.

I curve my tail around the front and slide it between her thighs, teasing her entrance with the ribbed tip. She's already hot and slippery for me, her soft little moans making me so fucking hard it hurts.

Still fisting her hair, I slide my free hand down her belly, lower, gently rubbing her clit with the pad of my finger.

"More," she whispers. "I need more."

"I know you do, witchling. I know." I drag a claw over her clit, a light tease that has her panting again. Then I slide my tail inside her, curling the tip to hit that perfect spot, thrusting in and out, in and out, making her feel every thick, ribbed inch.

Before us, Jude grabs Alonzo Florentine by the back of the neck, hauling him to his feet. The broken body can't even stand on his own.

"Take it," I command my little witch. "Take this tail and show me how badly you need to come."

"Please," she murmurs, rocking her hips to take me in deeper, to increase the friction. "It feels so... so fucking good."

Jude's eyes find mine across the cold, concrete space.

His cock is hard, his muscles twitching with the need to kill, the need to fuck, the need to spill one more drop of blood.

"Do it," West grinds out. "Fucking do it."

He drags the blade across the Alonzo's throat. A dark, wet gash splits the skin. The mage chokes out his last breath, and Jude drops his lifeless corpse to the ground.

Westlyn gasps, a shudder wracking her body, but it's not from horror or shock.

The scent of her need is making me dizzy.

I increase the pressure on her clit, rubbing harder, faster, shoving my tail deeper inside her as she writhes and moans, chasing that pure, white-hot wave that's so damn close we can all taste it.

"You're so wet, witchling. So hot for me."

"Please. I can't... I can't take it. I need more," she begs. "Everything inside me is burning for it."

I release her hair and drag my hand down her spine, down to the soft curve of her ass, my fingers kneading her flesh.

"Here?" I say, squeezing hard. "Is this where you want me? Inside this tight little ass?"

Jude grabs a fistful of Jacob Pomeroy's hair and hauls him up, his bloodied, toeless feet an inch off the ground.

"Yes," West says, a moan and a whisper both, and I unfurl my tongue, licking a hot path across the scars on her lower back.

W, I mark with my tongue, followed by a straight lick for the *I*.

C, a gentle tease, and three long licks for the *K*.

E, sideways, down, over and back again.

D, a lick and a swirl and one more feather-soft kiss at the end of it all...

And then I shove my tongue in her ass.

"Holy *fuck*," she gasps.

Jude watches us, his breath ragged, his eyes glazed with lust as I lick and suck and devour our hot little witch, my tongue so deep inside that tight little hole I can feel the ridges of my own tail as it fucks her slick pussy, harder, faster, my fingers circling her clit...

"Right there," she breathes, a tremor rolling up her thighs. "Right there!"

Jude brings the blade to the mage's throat. A quick, deep slice. A growl of vengeance. A spray of blood. The sound of a body dropped, a skull splitting open on a concrete floor.

"Yes!" my witchling cries out. "Goddess, yes!" She shudders around my tail and tongue and fingers, coming with a force that seems to ripple across the entire building, the tools clattering against the counter, the rusty chains moaning on their hooks, the whole of fucking New York City damn near falling down around us.

And all the while, my witchling keeps her gaze locked on Jude.

Minutes. Hours.

And then, when she finally stops quaking, when I finally pull out of her and help her back into her pants, when her heartbeat finally slows and I'm certain she's back in her body, I stand up to my full height and look once more at my oldest friend, my gargoyle brother.

And a bolt of fear like nothing I've ever felt before shoots straight down the middle of my heart.

It's not the manic look in his crazy, cobalt blue eyes.

It's not the blade still clutched in his hand, slick with the blood of two shadow magic society mages.

It's not the gore dripping down his face, or the two crimson pools spreading out from the bodies, lying in a heap on the concrete.

It's their skin.

There, covering every visible inch, the markings West carved glow with that same unsettling silver-white light. Hundreds of them, each one pulsing like a heartbeat.

There was no way to see it before, when they were just a collection of bloody slashes on already bloodied flesh. But now, with each one glowing like a winter moon, there's no mistaking what they are.

"Auggie," she breathes. "Did I... Did I do that?"

I wrap my hand around the back of her neck, trying to calm her with a gentle touch. "Yes."

"What... what are they?"

I close my eyes, wishing I could unsee it all. Wishing she'd never come here tonight. Wishing I didn't have to tell her the truth.

But I can't.

She did.

And I do.

"Fuck," Jude whispers, crouching down for a closer look, all his earlier lust and rage replaced with pure terror as the realization settles over him, too. "Fucking hell."

"Auggie?"

"They're runes, West," I finally say, that cold, terrifying wind howling inside my chest. "Dark fae runes."

CHAPTER TWENTY-THREE

DRAEGAN

The woman Jude's carrying across the underground parking garage is barely recognizable as the woman I delivered here earlier.

Blood is smeared across her forehead, her eyes wide with shock. Even before they reach me, I can tell she's trembling from head to toe.

Fear slams into my chest, and I'm out of the car in a heartbeat, my glamour dropping away, claws bursting free as I round the other side. "Fucking Jude! What the fuck happened?"

Ignoring me, he opens the passenger door and lowers her onto the seat, tucking her legs in. "There you are, darling. Safe and sound now."

Staring blankly out the windshield, teeth chattering, Westlyn nods, but doesn't utter a word. I'm not even sure she realizes where she is. Who she's with.

He kisses her blood-stained face, leaving another smear of it in his wake, and gently closes the door behind her.

The moment he turns to face me, I've got him shoved back against the door, seconds away from tearing out his throat. "You were *supposed* to look after her. You assured me—"

"Relax." Jude raises his hands in surrender, his own face so filthy with blood I'm not sure I'd recognize him if not for the wild blue eyes—eyes that are now glaring at me, as if *I'm* the one in the wrong here. "Things just got a bit intense, is all."

"Intense? She's practically catatonic!"

"She's tougher than she looks, Draegan. Give our girl a bit of credit, will you?" He flashes his manic grin, then extricates himself from my hold and heads back toward the door that leads inside. "Got some loose ends to tie up here, then we'll be along. See you at home for the recap later."

He disappears inside the building, not giving me a chance to get in another word.

Probably for the best. Right now, Westlyn is the priority.

I'll deal with Jude later.

Taking a deep breath, I slip back into my glamour for the long drive home and get behind the wheel.

"Miss Avery, are you all right?" I ask softly, but the girl doesn't acknowledge me. Doesn't even blink. "Westlyn, I understand you've just been through something traumatic, but I need to know if you're hurt so I can assess your wounds."

She shakes her head, still shivering.

I turn the heat on full blast, aiming all the vents her way. Then, gesturing toward the cup holder, "I brought you a treat from Stella's. Still hot, if you want it."

"Th-thank you," she finally whispers, and I'm about ready to weep in relief that she's actually speaking again.

But she's far from well—barely manages to keep the cup steady as she brings it to her pale lips.

"Tell me what you need, love," I whisper. "Tell me what to do. I can't fix it if I don't know what—"

"Draegan, just... just drive. Please."

I watch her for another beat, then nod and maneuver us out of the garage.

We ride in silence through the annoying late-night traffic clogging the city streets. Once we get through the Lincoln Tunnel, the road finally opens up, and Westlyn blows out a long, shuddering breath.

"Thanks for the latte." She finishes the last of it and sticks the empty cup back in the holder. "I needed that."

Her voice is steady now, but her hands are still trembling.

Noticing me looking at them, she clenches them into fists and shoves them into her coat pockets.

"Maybe I should've gotten you decaf," I say.

"It's not the coffee, Draegan. It's... *damn it*." She squeezes her eyes shut, as if she's trying to erase whatever the hell she witnessed tonight. "I'm losing it. I'm seriously losing it and I can't even remember everything that happened and I feel like the walls are closing in and I can't breathe and I—"

"*Westlyn.*" I slide my hand behind her neck, giving her a gentle squeeze. My touch is steady, but inside my blood is simmering again, my frustration with Jude tempered only by my concern for the girl beside me. "Tell me what happened."

"They were here... The guys who..." She trails off into a sob, her shoulders hitching.

"I know, love. I'm sorry. Seeing them again must've been..." My other hand tightens around the wheel, knuckles white. "...difficult."

She takes another moment to gather herself. Then, "It wasn't, though," she whispers. "Not... not like I thought. Is that weird?"

"Confronting the men who terrorized you... I don't imagine there's a rule book. Whatever you felt is completely valid."

"It's just... I've been having nightmares about what they did to me for a decade. Seeing them again... I figured I'd freak out. Like it would bring everything rushing right back. Instead, I was oddly calm. Cold, even. Jude led me into this slaughterhouse room, and suddenly there they were, slumped on the floor. Meat hooks dangled from the ceiling. There was a big grinder thing, too."

"I'm familiar with the layout." I don't mention how

often I've been there. The packing plant has been one of Jude's favorite "worksites" since we purchased it in the mid-fifties.

"Jude and Auggie had already worked them over pretty good," she continues. "There was a lot of blood. I've never seen skin so pale. I... I knew they didn't have long to live."

I continue massaging her neck with a light touch, a million questions racing through my mind, but I don't dare voice them now. Don't dare scare her back into silence.

"The whole drive down tonight, I kept thinking about what I wanted to say to them. What final words I'd leave them with, knowing mine would likely be the last they ever heard. I wanted them to know I was still standing, despite what they did to me. Still fighting. I wanted them to look me in the eye and know it was my turn now—that *I* was the reason for *their* suffering. I asked them if they knew who I was. I showed them my scars. But when the time came for my big speech, all the words I'd rehearsed in my mind just... just vanished." She wipes a tear from her blood-streaked face. "Ten years ago, they stole my dignity. Obliterated any sense of safety I had. Over and over, I begged them to stop. I begged them for my life. I screamed for them until my throat was raw. Jake called me a wicked little whore tonight. And in that moment, I realized I didn't want to give them another fucking *word*. I wanted to give them pain."

We're practically alone on the highway now, the hum of the tires on the road a comforting din, her heartbeat slow and steady once more.

"Good girl," I whisper, a surge of pride welling up inside.

"I found a dagger—a curved blade so sharp it could split dust motes. As soon as I wrapped my hand around the grip, a strange feeling came over me, just like earlier when I drew the Ace of Swords card. From that moment on, I was on autopilot. I remember kneeling before them. I remember pressing the knife to Jake's throat. I said something about making their last moments agonizing, and how that would be nothing compared to what they'd suffer at *his* hands... His? I'm not even sure who I meant. It didn't feel like any of those words even came from me. And then I just... blacked out."

She's silent for so long, I begin to worry she's slipping under again. My hand tightens around the back of her neck, and then—finally—she turns to me and says, "The next thing I remembered, I was across the room in Auggie's arms, begging him to... to touch me while Jude finished the job with the mages. I watched him slit their throats, but then something changed... All of a sudden, all I could see were the runes. Their bodies were carved with them. Every inch of visible skin... And every rune pulsed with a strange silver light."

"Runes? But... *You* carved them?"

"I wouldn't have believed it if Auggie and Jude didn't swear it was me. It's like I was in a trance the whole time. None of us even noticed what they were until that very instant, when they started glowing."

"Did they say what the runes were? Did you recognize them? Some sort of witchcraft, or—"

"Fae," she whispers. "Dark fae. That's as far as Auggie could tell. He took pictures, hoping Rook can figure it out. By then, I was too exhausted and freaked out to pay attention."

I sense her heartbeat kicking up again, so I run my hand over her head and say softly, "Don't worry, love. It's over now. I'm taking you home. I'll draw you a hot bath and fix you some herbal tea, if you'd like."

Again, she falls silent.

Again, I want to hang Jude upside down by his tail and beat him like a fucking piñata.

I know it was important for her to be there tonight— she convinced me of that when she told me about her Tarot cards. I wasn't thrilled with the idea, but ultimately, I hoped that seeing her attackers take their final breaths would give her some closure.

Jude and Augustine never should've let it go so far.

"Draegan?" she asks, her voice small and frightened, and when I turn and meet her gaze again, her eyes are wide with some new terror. "I think something's wrong with me. I don't know what it is, but carving those runes... I think it changed something inside me. Unlocked something that probably should've stayed behind bars."

"Nothing is wrong with you," I say. "Violence like that, no matter how deserving our victims... It takes something from us, Westlyn. What the others and I do... The things we..." I swallow the sudden tightness in my throat, centuries of pain and anguish and regret and guilt, every memory a blade that never dulls. "It's not the sort of life I'd *ever* want for you."

"But that's the thing," she whispers. "It didn't take something from me."

A flash of eerie, otherworldly light pulses through her eyes—so quickly I'd have missed it if I'd blinked.

"It... it gave something back." She closes her eyes, and a chill slithers across the back of my neck, making the hairs stand on end. "Something I think I've been missing my entire life."

I don't know how to respond to that. To *any* of this— the runes, her temporary memory loss, the strange light in her eyes, all the things she's feeling. Before I can even *attempt* to find the right thing to say, she's trembling again, her breathing heavy and uneven, her heart stuttering.

"Breathe, love," I whisper, brushing my knuckles across her cheek. "Just breathe."

"I'm trying," she pants, "but I... I can't catch my breath. I can't... Draegan, I can't breathe!"

"You can. Just focus on my touch. Right here, Miss Avery." I lower my hand and press it to her abdomen. "Feel that?"

She grips my forearm with both hands. "Y-yes."

"Good. I want you to take a few nice, deep breaths into your lower belly, as if you're trying to breathe through my hand."

She obeys, her stomach rising and falling beneath my touch, but it's not enough. She's still breathing too fast, her body trembling again, her heart rate skyrocketing.

Fucking Jude.

"There, there, love," I say softly, fighting to keep my voice calm and steady. "The worst is over now, and whatever comes next, we'll deal with it together, one step at a time. For now, I just need you to keep breathing. Keep focusing on my voice and my touch, and breathe. Can you do that for me?"

With another shuddering breath, she nods.

"Good girl." I continue to stroke her stomach, keeping one hand on the wheel, my gaze darting from the highway to Westlyn and back again. "That's it. Just breathe. You're okay. See? Everything's just fine."

I'm not sure which of us I'm trying to convince.

Either way, I don't think it's working.

"You're okay," I say again.

"I... I don't think I am."

"Do I need to stop?"

"No!" Her grip on my forearm tightens. "Don't stop! Please don't stop touching me!"

My jaw clenches tight. "I meant the *car*, Miss Avery. Do I need to stop the car and—"

"No. You just need to..." She takes another gasping breath, then turns to look at me again full on, her eyes glassy and far away. "Touch me, Draegan," she whispers, guiding my hand lower, her hips arching closer.

Is she really asking what I think she's asking?

"Miss Avery, I—"

"I need you to touch me," she says, her voice a desperate plea. "It's the same thing that happened with Auggie, and I... I know I sound like a crazy person and I'll explain later but right now just... Do this for me? Please?"

"No. Absolutely not."

"Auggie tried to help... I thought I was okay, but I guess it wasn't enough... I'm on fire. Everything inside me is burning up and... Please, Draegan. I need it. I need *you*, just this once."

Fuck.

The heat of her touch, the urgency in her words, the soft breathy sounds she's making beside me... All of it is conspiring to ruin me, just as *she* is conspiring to ruin me.

I don't know what the fuck has come over her, but there's no mistaking what she's asking for now. *Begging* for. Every instinct I possess is telling me to pull away. To put both hands *firmly* on the wheel and shut my damn mouth until we're safely back at the manor, where she can go to her room, I can go to mine, and we can both forget this moment *ever* came to pass.

But then, there it is. One last breathy plea whispering through her lips. One last desperate tug on my wrist.

And no matter how terrible an idea I *know* this is, I'm powerless to refuse.

CHAPTER TWENTY-FOUR

DRAEGAN

"Do *not* read into this, little mortal," I say firmly, as if *she's* the one who needs the warning.

She shakes her head vehemently, the intensity in her eyes sealing a promise I'm not sure I want her to keep.

"Unzip your jacket and lean back," I whisper. "And close your eyes."

Because if I have to see the look in them when I make you come, I'm fairly certain I won't be able to stop with merely a touch...

Once again, she obeys my commands without question.

After another silent argument with myself about crossing lines and making foolish mistakes and spending every night for the rest of bloody *eternity* alternately regretting and fantasizing about this moment, I hit the button to recline her seat back a bit, and then...

Fuck.

I finally give in to her demands.

It starts with a gentle caress, fingers spanning her taut stomach. She's only wearing a sports bra underneath the jacket, her hoodie gone.

"Thank you," she whispers, and my touch circles lower, lower still, until I'm finally dipping inside the waistband of her loose pants, skimming over the lacy undergarments beneath.

Heat radiates from between her thighs, a tantalizing invitation I can't resist, and I glide even lower, the pad of my middle finger brushing the lace over her clit, making her shudder, making myself nearly drive off the damn road. She's so soft and warm and... *fucking hell*, the scent of her has my cock stirring to vicious life, wishing like hell I could shed the human glamor, give the gargoyle free rein, and just fucking *claim* her.

"Draegan..." Her voice is a quiet sigh as she clutches my forearm and urges me lower, already arching her hips for more—more of the very touch I've been fantasizing about since I first took her into my arms atop the bell tower, drew her close, and leaped into the night.

"Just relax, little mortal," I whisper, finally working my way inside her panties. "I've got you."

"Thank you. I swear this isn't—"

"Shh. No more talking. Just spread your legs for me, love."

I'm the one who's desperate now, aching to slide into her, to feel her body clench around my fingers until she's quaking and gasping and...

Fuck, it's wrong. Every one of my dark, depraved thoughts is wrong. I know she wants this release—needs it—but she's no longer the only one harboring such cravings.

My whole body is buzzing with it—the reckless, urgent *need* to make the little mortal come unraveled for me.

The moment her thighs part, all sense of right and wrong evaporates, and all I've got left is throbbing balls, a hard-on I'll be walking off for hours, and a foolish, fevered dream to hear *my* name in that lush little mouth.

Not Jude's. Not Augustine's.

Mine.

"That's it. Good girl." I dip a finger into her wet heat, then another, pumping her slowly, deliberately, my words no more than a murmur in the darkness. "I want you to *feel* this, little mortal. Feel every inch of my fingers sinking into your wet pussy... Dragging out slowly, then pushing back in... In, and out... In, and out... Mmm, just like that."

She squirms in the seat, her soft little gasps doing absolutely *nothing* to relieve the endless ache in my balls, but I don't dare stop.

"Does that feel good?" I whisper.

"Goddess, yes. The way you touch me is... *Draegan.*"

My name ends in a soft moan, the sound of it like a hot fist around my cock. Fuck *me*, her body is so responsive, so alive, every part of her primed and ready for this. Ready for me.

I stroke her again, thrusting inside her as she urges me deeper, losing herself in this moment, this shared forbidden pleasure as we drive on through the night, our hearts beating in tandem, the entire world vanishing around us until there's only us, only this heat, only this ecstasy.

Touching her like this, making her writhe and moan for me, taking away her pain for even just a *moment*...

I've never felt anything like it.

If I could, I'd make it last an eternity.

But it's not long before I'm as greedy to make her come as she is to fucking feel it. A slow tremble is already working its way up her thighs, her breath quickening with every pulse of my fingers.

"You want to come for me, don't you, love?" I whisper. "You're so close. So hot and wet and eager."

"Draegan," she breathes. "Please."

I curl my fingers and fuck her faster, harder, hitting that spot inside her that makes her gasp, the heel of my hand grinding against her clit, bringing her closer, closer to that frantic spiral, that white-hot starburst that's just out of reach...

"Draegan," she cries out, and the sound of it is *perfect*, her fingernails digging into my arm, heat spreading across her chest, back arching off the seat, hot flesh quivering around my fingers and then...

Oh, fuck... my sweet little mortal just fucking *shatters*.

~

Silence descends once more, nothing but the twin beating of wild hearts, the soft sound of her breath, the same hum of the tires on the road.

When I finally find the courage to meet her eyes again, the sight of her scrapes against the softest parts of my heart, leaving it raw and aching. Tears streak her face, her eyes shining with a mix of gratitude and confusion.

"I'm... I'm sorry," she whispers. "I feel like maybe I crossed a line... I shouldn't have asked you to... I don't know what came over me."

"Are you hurt?" I ask, barely following her words, her tears so raw and unexpected I can only assume the worst. "Did I... Was I too rough?"

"No, it's nothing like that. It was amazing. Perfect. I'm just... super emotional, all of a sudden. Everything's kind of... I think I'm just crashing." The softest, sweetest laugh finally bubbles up through her lips, and again I find myself sighing in relief. "Goddess, I don't know why I'm being so *extra* right now. All aboard the hot mess express!"

"Miss Avery, I... Westlyn. You've got nothing to apologize for. I'm the one who..." I blow out a breath, trying to wrangle my thoughts. Then, softer, "I just want to be sure you're all right."

"Not really. But I'm a hell of a lot better than I was when I first got into this car, so that's saying something, right?" Her smile is warm and genuine, but all I can manage is a quick nod in response.

"Close your eyes and rest," I say, reaching over to pull

the jacket tight around her once more. "We'll be home before you know it."

"Okay." She's silent for a few beats, and then... "Um, Draegan?"

"Yes, love?"

"Thank you," she whispers. "That was... Yeah. Thank you."

With one more smile and a barely contained yawn, she finally settles back against the seat and closes her eyes. Moments later, her breathing becomes deep and even, her mouth parted, the cutest little snores escaping her lips.

I'd laugh if I could, but right now, all I can think about is the scent of her desire filling the small space of the car, and my fingers curled around the steering wheel, still shimmering and wet from making her come.

That was... Yeah. Thank you...

Bloody *hell*, I want to lick her off my skin to savor the taste of her, but I don't dare. Not like this. Not while she's asleep beside me, trusting me to take her home.

I stole a brief taste of her once before—the night I rushed into her room thinking she was being attacked, only to realize I'd just caught her touching herself. I sucked her fingers into my mouth, swirling my tongue over every inch, but that was merely a power game—a dick move intended to intimidate her into submission.

Some power move. The only thing I managed to accomplish that night was giving myself an all-too-brief taste of something I could never *really* have. Not that night. Not tonight. Not ever.

She's right—we did cross a line tonight. Both of us. And the more I allow those lines to blur, the greater the danger for her.

We need to stay focused on keeping her safe. On breaking our curse. On eliminating her enemies.

Jude and Augustine are fools to believe they can have it all, *do* it all. Hell, they're already falling for her.

And love? That's something *none* of us are allowed to want.

We don't deserve it, and even if we did?

We simply can't have it.

So now, with nothing but her soft snores and my own spiraling thoughts to keep me company, I grip the wheel, ignoring the hot, slippery feel of her on my fingers, and ferry us home.

The moment we're back at Blackmoor Manor, I drop my glamour and exit the car, heading around to the passenger side where the little mortal is still fast asleep. I scoop her into my arms and gather her close, and for the briefest moment, she stirs, her eyes fluttering open to gaze up at me in the moonlight.

A smile touches her lips—the kind of smile that could melt my heart if I let it.

"For a guy who pretends not to like me very much," she says dreamily, "you sure have a knack for saving me."

Her smile lingers for another heartbeat, and then it's gone, sleep pulling her under once more. She rests her head against my chest, and I wrap my arms tighter around her, pressing my lips to the top of her head and breathing in her scent.

My protective instincts surge, but I hardly need the internal reminder. *Nothing* is more important to me than her wellbeing. It's the only reason I gave in to her wishes tonight. She needed my help, and I granted it.

Oh, yes. You're such a noble, selfless gargoyle, Caldwell. Really making the hard sacrifices tonight, aren't you?

Ignoring the voice of reason echoing through my skull, I carry her into the manor and up the stairs. But I bypass her bedroom, along with Augustine's and Jude's and Rook's. Instead, I carry her to the very last suite at the end of the hall—mine.

With a soft but efficient touch, I wash her face and hands with a warm, wet cloth, then remove her blood-stained clothing and dress her in one of my T-shirts.

Through all of it, she barely stirs.

And then, with one more soft kiss against her forehead, I gently tuck her into my bed.

Mine.

I tell myself it's because I don't know whether she'd prefer Jude's or Auggie's bed tonight, and I don't want to make any assumptions.

Mine.

I tell myself it's because I need to keep an eye on her to ensure she doesn't suffer any more ill effects from her ordeal at the meat packing plant.

Mine.

I tell myself a hundred other things—everything but the right thing, the true thing, the thing that keeps whispering through the barren halls of my heart.

Mine.

Ultimately, I settle on a slight variation of that truth, if only because I can't bring myself to admit the rest.

When it comes to this girl, there's *nothing* I won't do to keep her safe. To keep her alive. To keep her happy and whole and protected from all the monsters outside these walls.

Because there will come a day—sooner than I want and sooner than she deserves—when Westlyn Avery will once again find herself alone in a world that doesn't fucking deserve her.

CHAPTER TWENTY-FIVE

WESTLYN

Darkness takes me, sweeping me into another vicious dreamscape...

Rook's arms tighten around my waist, my back pressed firmly against his muscled chest as we fly over New York City.

Manhattan is in ruins.

"Where... where is everyone?" I ask.

"Most of the supernaturals fled. Few humans survived the initial attack, but those that did... It's not pretty, West."

He banks a hard right, and I glance down through the clouds of dark, oily smoke, catching sight of a small group of people.

They're shackled, chained together, bleeding as they march down Broadway, whips at their backs.

"We have to help them, Rook! We have to do something!"

"We can't, West. We need to get to the portal. It's our only shot at getting you out of here."

He banks again, spiraling us up into the clouds, then tucking his wings in close and zooming south.

There, in the distance, I see it.

The last building standing, a lone sentry in a field of concrete-and-steel corpses.

The Blackmoor Capital building.

We land on the roof, and Rook sets me on my feet. His glasses are smudged with soot and grime. I reach up and remove them, trying to clean them on my shirt, but all I'm doing is smearing the dirt around.

"I'm so sorry, West," Rook says. "It wasn't supposed to be this way. Not for you."

I glance up into his honey-colored eyes, the pain so endless. So deep.

"I never even kissed you," he says, cupping my cheek. His palm is rough, the skin warm. "I should have... When I... I'm... sorry..." The light dims from his eyes. His face slackens, his touch turning stiff against my cheek.

"Rook? Rook!" I put my hands on his chest, but there's no heartbeat to be found. Nothing but cold, hard stone. "No!"

I drop his glasses and beat my fists against his chest until my hands are raw and bleeding. I scream for Auggie and Jude, for Draegan, for the goddess.

No one hears me. No one comes.

All around me, the city crumbles and burns.

I don't know where the guys are. Where this so-called portal is, or where it was supposed to take us.

I only know that I'm alone. That the men I love are gone.

I close my eyes and fall to my knees on the rooftop, a howl of agony shredding my throat.

Beneath me, the building rumbles. A thousand window-panes shatter, glass crashing to the street below. There's a resounding crack, and when I finally get to my feet and open my eyes again, the sight before me obliterates what's left of my heart.

Rook. My sweet, naughty professor. My favorite genius and book nerd and kind-hearted soulmate... Is nothing more than a pile of broken stone at my feet.

I can't breathe. I can't breathe. I can't...

"Do not despair, little one. Everything is unfolding as it should be." The dark voice behind me reverberates through my chest, his hand an icy grip on my shoulder. I whirl around and come face-to-face with the most terrifying man I've ever encountered. Tall and thin, with pale, shimmery skin and midnight black hair that hangs past his shoulders. His silver eyes glitter with malice.

I've never encountered the dark fae before, but I know at once that's exactly what he is.

"Let me go!" I jerk free from his grasp and stumble backward. The fae vanishes into thin air, only for another pair of arms to wrap around me from behind, pinning me in place.

Unlike the fae, this monster is familiar to me. His touch makes my skin crawl, bile rising in my throat.

His voice leaks into my mind, poking and prodding. Terrifying.

Zorakkov, demon prince of hell.

My fingers twitch, desperate to feel the athame again, just like on our wedding night. To shove it into his throat.

But there's no athame here. Only rot. Only death.

He loosens his hold, and I turn around to face him. He's wearing Hunter's body, but those eyes are pure demon—a dark, soulless black that shines with pride as he takes in the surrounding ruins.

"It's beautiful, is it not?" his voice snakes through my mind, his lips unmoving.

Ignoring the question, I turn away from him and walk toward the edge of the roof. There's a sound behind me— the familiar clip-clop of a trotting horse—and I turn to find a white stallion approaching me.

How he got on the roof is a mystery, but I sense he's not here to hurt me. I hold out my hand, and he sniffs my palm. Gray spots dust his muzzle like tiny freckles.

I know this horse.

"Shoot the Messenger," I say softly, stroking his flank. I used to have a picture of him on my dresser in Brooklyn. My father took me to the races once, and he let me pick the winning horse to bet on. Messenger lost, but we still stayed after for a photo. "What are you doing here, buddy? It isn't safe."

He whinnies and rears up on his hind legs, crashing back down before me again, his big brown eyes imploring me. *Remember me*, he seems to be saying. *Remember my name.*

I'm about to promise him that I will, but then he's gone, vanishing, just like the fae.

Zorakkov is standing in his place again, his black eyes boring through me.

"This is all for us, my love," he says, his thoughts simply appearing in my head, as if he planted them long ago and now they're finally blooming. "A shining achievement. A grand monument to honor the joining of our two powerful bloodlines."

His words unleash a new fury inside me. "I would rather die than align with the monster responsible for this. You... murderer!"

His dark chuckle rolls across my mind, making me shiver. Zorakkov's black eyes blaze with delight.

I try to back away from him, but he won't give me an inch. He matches every pace, kicking pieces of Rook off the building as he stalks closer and closer.

With a final crunch, he stamps on the forgotten glasses.

It's that. The sight of them—that one small thing that was such a part of Rook. That one small thing, smashed and ruined... It brings the grief back full-force, a tsunami of pain that barrels into me and steals the breath from my lungs.

I'm on my knees again, tears spilling down my face, but Zorakkov only smiles.

Crouching before me, he catches my tears with his

thumbs and says, "I would love to take credit for this masterpiece, but my powers are not that strong."

"Not that strong?" I shout. "You leveled the entire city! My city! You wiped my home off the fucking map! You murdered the men I love!"

He shakes his head, and for a moment, his demon eyes shift to human. Hunter's eyes, the dull brown I remember from our wedding night.

For the briefest instant, the demon is gone, and Hunter looks down on me with pity.

"No, Westlyn Avery," he says plainly. "You did."

"No!" A devastating pain knifes through my skull, and I bolt up in bed with a gasp, clutching my head in my hands as the real world comes back into focus. "Holy shit. Holy fucking shit..."

Tears leak from my eyes, my heart bursting with grief, but... no.

A nightmare. Just another nightmare.

Goddess, it was so real.

I close my eyes and rub my temples, the pain in my head slowly receding. When I finally feel like I can move again without unleashing another migraine, I slip out from under the blankets and dangle my legs over the edge of the bed.

Outside, the early evening sky is streaked with sherbet-colored light, a much lovelier wake-up call than the terrifying nightmare.

Only... I don't recognize the view.

In fact, I don't recognize the bed, either, or the T-shirt I'm wearing...

Draegan. His scent washes over me—a summer wind whipping across the wildest ocean. One by one, the memories from last night flicker through my mind.

Jude and Auggie.

The mages.

The blood.

The dagger, the runes.

Draegan, trying to keep me calm on the drive home...

Draegan, his warm hand on my belly, his soothing voice urging me to breathe, just breathe...

Draegan, answering my desperate plea...

I need you to touch me... Do this for me... Please...

Heat floods my core, my heart stuttering as my body remembers his expert touch. His control. His filthy words as he brought me closer and closer...

I want you to feel this, little mortal. Feel every inch of my fingers sinking into your wet pussy...

In, and out... Mmm, just like that...

You want to come for me, don't you, love?

Oh, holy hell. Yes, I *did* want to come for him. I don't know what came over me—not in the plant, not in the car after, but I needed it. I was so hungry—starved for it—I truly believed I would die without that release.

And oh, *yes*, Daddy Drae delivered on that offer. With nothing more than his fingers. I didn't even take my clothes off, and he didn't even take his eyes off the road. But the way he touched me... Fuck, it was like a thousand epic finger-bangs all rolled into one earth-shattering, back-bending, mouth-watering—

Stop. Stop thinking about it, because it's never going to happen again.

I hop to my feet and jog in place, trying to shake those memories right out of my...

Yeah. Right out of *that*.

Hey. The body remembers, people. The body remembers.

But in this case, it's nothing more than a pointless fantasy that *needs* to be forgotten, pronto. Draegan doesn't look at me that way—not like Jude and Auggie. Even Rook. As shy as he comes off, it's clear he's open to something more between us. Maybe not tonight, but one night.

Daddy Drae, on the other hand...

I bring the collar of his T-shirt to my nose, breathing in the scent. It's freshly laundered, but I can still smell him. He's in the very fabric, the sheets, the air.

He must've put me in his bed last night. In his shirt. I don't remember that part.

I lower the shirt again, and my eyes land on the night-stand beside the bed. There's a small ceramic dish—plain white, with a scalloped edge. The kind of thing you might use to hold your wedding ring while you do dishes or roll cookie dough.

This dish doesn't hold jewelry, though. Just a pale gray stone naturally shaped like a heart. It's about the size of a golf ball. I pick it up and turn it toward the window, the fading light illuminating a set of initials carved into the back.

A.C., it looks like, but it's hard to tell. The stone has been worn smooth on this side, almost as if it was polished in a tumbler.

Or by the worrying of a thumb, I realize, suddenly picturing Draegan holding this stone, rubbing his thumb back and forth over the grooved letters, thinking about whoever gave it to him. The C could be for Caldwell.

Did he... *Goddess*. Did he have a wife?

A strange mix of emotion washes through me—heartache and jealousy. Grief. Even fear that a man like him could still have a soft, breakable heart inside.

I've only ever known him as Draegan, the stern, commanding, often pig-headed gargoyle who loves to tell me no and only occasionally shows a human side.

Like last night.

But he *was* human once, I remind myself. A man, probably in his forties. A man who may have loved...

And very probably lost.

I rub my thumb over the smooth stone, a chill skittering down my spine.

I set it back in the dish.

It's not for me to touch. It's not for me to even mention.

Blinking away fresh tears, I rise from the bed and head to my room to shower and dress, eager to scrub the remnants of the mage blood from under my fingernails.

Even more eager to head out to the library.

Rook. I need to find Rook. I need to see him with my own eyes and feel his warm embrace and know, without a doubt, that he's okay.

CHAPTER TWENTY-SIX

ROOK

The moment the sun sets behind Blackmoor Manor tonight, Jude and Draegan are in flight.

After everything that went down at the meat packing plant last night, I knew they would be. Jude was anxious to follow up on Conrad Nesterman—aka Full Metal Jacket. The name checked out—I was able to pull up his address, along with his family contacts and police record. His rap sheet was even longer than the other two mages'. Real fucking prince, this one.

Tonight's particular mission is a fact-finding fly-by *only*, and Draegan insisted on accompanying him to make sure our resident psycho sticks to the plan. After what they did to Florentine and Pomeroy, we need to lie low before the next round of interrogations, which will likely include Pomeroy's mother and this Nesterman asshole. Two mage buddies going off-grid aren't likely to raise any alarms—not for a few days, at least. But if half the shadow magic society starts vanishing without explanation? We've already got our hands full running Forsythe and Detective Reedsy in circles over West's "disappearance" and the fire, not to mention the stolen Codex.

With Jude and Drae down in Bayside scoping out Metal's residence, Auggie and I decided to stay at the manor with West tonight. I haven't seen her since the whole thing went down with the mages, but apparently she was in pretty rough shape. She was still asleep in Drae's bed when I woke up, so that's where I left her.

In the hour or so since then, Auggie and I—under the close supervision of Huxley and Lucinda—have been keeping busy snooping through the texts, photos, and voice-mails on the cell phones they took from Pomeroy and Florentine.

Between that evidence and the details Auggie shared with me about last night, a picture is starting to emerge.

But that's *all* it's doing—starting. It's way too soon to throw out those old favorite words of mine, certainty and determination. So far, all we've been able to *determine* with *certainty* is this:

The shadow magic society web is even more dark and tangled than any of us could've imagined, and Archmage Forsythe's got his sticky hands on every fucking strand.

～

"*There's* our girl," Auggie says, a smile splitting his face as West finally enters the library. Her hair is wrapped up in a wet bun, her cheeks pink and freshly scrubbed, but her eyes are haunted.

We both rise from the library table to greet her, but she comes to me first, throwing her arms around me and pressing her ear to my chest.

She's trembling when she says, "Your heart's beating, thank the goddess."

I laugh, running a hand over her head. "It tends to do that."

"Not in my nightmare." Another shudder ripples through her, and then she finally pulls back to look at me. Her eyes rove my face, scrutinizing. "You sure you're okay?"

"I'm fine. It's you I'm worried about. You're not usually this jittery pre-caffeine."

She finally smiles, then blows out a sigh of relief. "All good. Just needed to feel you for myself."

"What about me, witchling?" Auggie laughs. "Don't you want to feel *me* for yourself, too?"

"Always." She tries to hug him too, but he doesn't give her a chance. Just picks her up and wraps those massive wings around her, planting a big, wet kiss on her mouth.

She squeals in his hold, but it quickly turns into a moan of pleasure that has my dick standing tall, wondering where the fire is and how he can get in on it.

But before I can let my mind wander too far off the

leash with *that* little fantasy, Auggie's setting her back on her feet again, his voice turning serious. "Are you still..."

"Not like I was, no." She blushes, then says, "I'm sorry I got so... intense. I don't know what came over me."

"I still think it was the shock of everything. Everyone processes things differently." He leans in for another kiss, but this time it's just a quick peck on the forehead. "Anyway, first order of business—almond joy latte."

A new smile brightens her face. "That would be *epic*."

"Did you eat?"

"Nope."

"I've got some muffins and croissants here, but I can make you a full spread in the main house if—"

"No, pastries sound perfect right about now. I could use the sugar."

Auggie returns a few minutes later with fresh lattes for all of us and a plate of pastries for West. He gives her a few minutes to get settled in, get a bit of sugar and caffeine in her veins, share an apple-blueberry muffin with her raven besties—the pair are more than happy to stash some crumbs under the table for later.

And then, it's time to debrief her on the intel they tortured out of the mages before she showed up at the facility last night. Namely, the fact that her stepmother was the puppet master behind the brutal train station attack that nearly killed her.

Hearing him talk about it again now has my jaw clenching, my claws itching to shred through flesh and bone. One glance at his hazel eyes—wild with the telling—and I know he's feeling the same way.

"So Eloise hired Jacob, Alonzo, and Full Metal Jacket to terrorize me?" she asks.

"That's what they said, yes," Auggie replies. "Our best guess based on everything the mages said and everything else we've been trying to put together..." He blows out a breath, shaking his head. "It seems she wanted you to live in a constant state of fear. Always looking over your shoulder, never feeling confident, never being able to trust anyone."

"Powerless," West says. "She wanted me to feel powerless, because being a witch born without magic isn't powerless enough."

"Apparently not for her," I say. "She was afraid of you, West. I'm sure of it. Maybe you don't have magic, but there has to be something else she was after... Something she either wanted to destroy or claim for herself."

"And she thought sending the teenage mutant ninja mages to rough me up was the way to go?" she asks.

"Not just them," Auggie says. "Chances are she was behind a lot of the other bullying you experienced, too. She couldn't afford to have you making friends or trusting you had backup. For whatever reason, she wanted you docile and ashamed. Primed—that was the word that fuckstain Pomeroy used."

"Primed." West shakes her head, a bitter laugh escaping. "So one day I'd grow up feeling so desperate and worthless, I wouldn't even question it when they sold me off to the Archmage. To their fucking demon pet."

"Apparently, she was playing the long game," I say. "Which makes sense. Whatever their plans are with Zorakkov, that couldn't have come together overnight."

"Those boys attacked me when I was in middle school. Middle school! So Eloise already knew me at least, what, seven years before she supposedly met my dad?"

"Longer than that, I'm afraid." I grab my tablet and pull up the records on Hunter's hospital treatments, giving her a refresher. "There's a very good chance Eloise was involved with that, even though she worked in pediatrics at the time. And a very good chance she knew exactly who you were, and exactly what she and the shadow magic society could use you for."

Her face pales, her eyes wide with new fright. "Guys. What if... what if she killed my mother?"

"You said your mom died giving birth to you," Auggie says.

"Yeah, that's what my dad told me. But he never wanted to talk about it. I don't know anything about the circumstances—did she bleed out? Was it something else?"

"The hospital records we found showed complications from childbirth as the cause of death," I say. "I haven't been able to find any autopsy records or official death certificate, but I'm still digging."

Auggie drains his latte, then says, "Look. It's pretty clear Eloise has been pulling the strings on some kind of bullshit dark mage plot for a *long* time. We're going to bust that plot wide open—every fucking detail, every summoning spell, every fucking shadow magic cocksucker involved. But we need to do this methodically, witchling. Rook's way. No jumping to conclusions and freaking out before we've got proof."

"Couldn't have said it better myself." I grin at him across the table, raising my mug in cheers. Then, to West, I say, "We don't know if Eloise plotted against your mother, or was just in the right place at the right time to take advantage of a newborn witch without magic and a newly grieving single father. All we know is what Pomeroy confessed— Eloise hired them to torment and bully you in some sort of bid to make you more docile. He speculated this was for the eventual demon binding, but again, even that's unproven until we get more intel."

"Intel we *could* get," she says with another sigh, "if Draegan would let me contact Eloise or my father."

"Which he won't," Auggie says, "and neither will we, so put it out of your head right now. We'll find another way. Jude and Draegan are already following up on the intel we got on Metal, so it's only a matter of time."

West nods, but her eyes are far away, her half-finished latte going cold on the table.

"Speaking of leads," Auggie says, getting to his feet, "Will you two be okay without me for a bit?"

"Why, where you off to?" I ask.

"Darkroom. I need to get started on the film rolls from last night—see if there's anything else we might've missed."

"Like my spooky dark-fae rune art?" West tries to laugh, but it sputters out fast. "Goddess, it's all still such a blur."

He puts his hands on her shoulders, giving her a reassuring squeeze. "We'll figure it out, witchling. This is just one more step in the process, okay? Rook can look at the pictures and give us a new perspective."

"Once we've got the photos," I say, "I can run them through a few programs to compare them with the fae literature we've got, see if we can start to piece together the meaning. Fae or not, runes are a form of language, and language can be translated."

West nods, her shoulders relaxing a bit.

"You good?" Auggie asks, leaning down to kiss the top of her head.

West looks at me across the table and smiles—a question. I smile back—an answer.

"We're good," West says.

"Okay." Auggie points at me. "Holler if you make any earth-shattering discoveries and/or either of you are overcome with the sudden, inexplicable need to get naked."

"You'll be the first to know," I say. "On both counts."

He leans down one more time, tilting her head back to press the softest kiss to her lips, lingering just long enough to make me wish we could all blow off the rest of the night and just... yeah. Be overcome with the sudden, inexplicable need to get naked.

West must be thinking something along the same lines, because the scent of her desire floods the room, and Auggie laughs.

"Careful, witchling," he teases. "Keep thinking thoughts like that, and you'll screw up Rook's concentration."

She laughs. "How do you know what my thoughts are,

perv?"

"Rook? You want to give her the gargoyle super-senses biology lesson again?" Auggie lets out another deep laugh, and then he's gone, heading off to his darkroom to reveal more of last night's mysteries.

Piece by piece, the puzzle comes together.

The mage attacks. The demon prince. The Codex. Our curse. Wild West herself, our fierce little witch—a mystery we never saw coming.

I clear away the mugs and plates, then return to find West curled up by the fire, a blanket wrapped around her shoulders, her eyes glassy and far away.

"You still thinking about Eloise?" I ask, taking the chair across from her.

"No. I was just trying to remember my nightmare." She draws the blanket closer. "It felt so real, Rook."

She tells me about it—the smoldering city, the dark fae, the demon. The random horse, and of course, my epic demise.

"I wouldn't read too much into it, Wild West." I reach across the space between us and squeeze her knee. "There's a lot going on in your life right now. Sounds like it all manifested in one hell of a scary dream."

"I know. It's just... Watching you basically die before my eyes?"

"I'm here now, very much alive, beating heart and all."

"All that stuff makes sense—my fears manifesting in nightmares. The horse is a wildcard, though." She laughs.

"Shoot the Messenger. I haven't thought about him in years."

"He's a real horse?"

She nods, a thin smile curving her lips. "My father... He wasn't always the worst human being on the planet. When I was about five or six, he took me to the races once. Made a whole day of it. He even let me pick the horse he bet on. I picked Shoot the Messenger because he had these really cute freckles." She laughs. "Yeah, that was the beginning and end of my illustrious gambling career. The horse came in dead last. I never went back to the track after that, but my father spent a lot of time there. He always bet on that same horse, even though he never won."

The fire pops, and she trails off into a sigh, bringing the blanket up to her chin.

"I think he wanted to be a good father, you know? But life just... It didn't work out the way he thought it would."

"Never does."

A tear spills down her cheek, but she wipes it away with the blanket.

"I wish I could hate him," she whispers. "It would make things so much easier."

"I know. But you loved him once. That's not a bond that's easy to break, whether it needs to be broken or not."

"Why did he keep me?" She meets my eyes, her own shining with raw pain.

"What do you mean?"

"If I was such a burden to him all those years, why didn't

he put me up for adoption? Why did he even take me out of the hospital? My mother had supposedly just died in child-birth. He could've just... just walked away, no strings. Left me in the care of the state." She shakes her head. "I'd say maybe he was trying to do the right thing—like maybe he didn't want me to end up in foster care or somewhere where I'd be abused or neglected—but isn't that the same thing as selling me to a demon?"

"I don't know, West," I say softly, feeling every one of her tears in my chest, a blade to my heart. It hits me all over again, like it has so many times over the centuries, and I can't decide what's worse:

Knowing you're completely unwanted from the start, or spending your life chasing after the little scraps of affection a negligent parent doles out, hoping against the odds this time it will last, this time it will be better, this time it will change... Only to have it all snatched away from you again.

"I don't pretend to understand your father's motives," I continue. "But you're *not* a burden." I cross the small space between us and kneel before her, cradling her face in my hands. "You're a gift, Westlyn Avery. A rare, magnificent gift. And I feel *damn* sorry for anyone who can't see that— especially a man like your father, who held you in his arms and watched you take your first few precious breaths, and still walked away in the end. And for what? One more night at the casino? One more—"

"Rook," she whispers, and I clamp my mouth shut, shaking my head.

"I'm sorry. I shouldn't have said—"

"No, you're right. The casino... My father was a *compulsive* gambler." Her brow furrows, the sadness fading from her eyes. "He gambled like it was his job, his passion, his whole damn *existence*."

"What are you saying?"

"Why would a compulsive gambler who planned his life around race schedules and casino hours keep betting on a losing horse?"

"*Compulsive* doesn't mean he was good at it. Didn't you say he lost all your family's money?"

"Yeah, but not because he didn't know how to play. He just never knew when to walk away. Horse racing is unpredictable, sure, but when a horse never wins a single race? Those are some tough odds to overcome. Only a complete fool would make that bet more than a handful of times."

"Maybe it was his way of... I don't know. Connecting with you, even after he fucked everything up."

She gets to her feet, pacing before the fire. "No. He only took me to the races that one time. He didn't even talk about it after that, really. I would just find the stubs lying around—that's how I knew who he'd bet on. Shoot the Messenger, every time." She stops pacing and glances up at me, her eyes bright. "What if he was trying to tell me something?"

"Like what?"

"I don't know," she says, already heading for the door. "But maybe we can figure it out. Be right back."

CHAPTER TWENTY-EIGHT

WESTLYN

I return to the library a few minutes later with another basket full of muffins I pilfered from the kitchen—apple cinnamon, this time—and a framed photo I dug out of one of the boxes Jude brought back from my bedroom in Brooklyn.

It had lived on my dresser all through my childhood—first in the front, where I'd see it every time I put away my clothes or got ready for the day. Over time, it slowly migrated to the back, pushed aside to make room for a new Tarot deck or a handful of rocks I found in the park or some cute little trinket Jean-Pierre brought me—his way of saying hello after a prolonged absence.

Eventually, I stopped noticing it—it was just part of the background of my childhood, like the Elmo stickers on my mirror or the lines on the closet wall where I tried to mark my own height with a pencil.

Even when I unpacked the boxes and set up my new room here at Blackmoor Manor, I barely paid it any mind—just stuck it in the discard box with a few other things from my childhood I no longer needed, and shoved it into the closet.

"This is him," I say now, showing Rook the photo—me, my father, and Shoot the Messenger.

Rook grins. "I'm quite sure I've never seen anything so adorable."

"He's pretty cute." I laugh. "It's the freckles, right? I told you. That's why I picked him."

He nudges my shoulder. "I was talking about the chubby little angel sitting on her father's shoulders."

"Oh, yes. Chubby little angel, that's me."

"You had that silver-and-raven hair even then."

"Just like my mom." I smile, my throat tightening with a familiar knot. "I've got her eyes, too."

"She must've been beautiful."

"Yeah." I stare at the photo for another moment—my huge, chubby-cheeked grin as I gazed adoringly at that horse. My father, his hands around my ankles, holding me in place. The horse standing next to us, not really caring one way or the other. "I don't even remember who took the photo. I just remember thinking my dad must be some sort of king, what with how many people he knew at the track. How they just let us back there like some kind of VIP guests."

There's nothing out of the ordinary about the photo

itself, but when I flip it over and pop it out of the frame, my heart leaps into my throat.

"Jackpot," I breathe. "No pun intended."

There's a flat, nondescript silver key taped inside the frame. And on the back of the photo, a message in my dad's sloppy scrawl.

Passing the key to Rook, I read the note. "Edgewater Raceway. Westlyn, Dad, and Shoot the Messenger."

"That's it?" Rook asks.

"Yep. Just the—wait." I bring the photo closer, tilting it toward the light. "There's more! It's in pencil, sort of underneath the ink.

"Can you make it out? We can put it under the microscope."

"No, I think I can read it. It says, 'Be good for Renni.'"

"Renni? Is that a person?"

"It's... yes!" The name unlocks a flood of memories. "Renni was an old witch on the Upper East Side—one of the healers my father used to bring me to when he was still trying to figure out why I didn't have magic. She was the only one I liked. She was always nice to me, and instead of poking me with hot needles or forcing me to drink nasty-tasting potions, she would just hang out and talk to me. She's the one who showed me how to read Tarot, actually— she used to let me play with her decks."

"Was she close with your father?" Rook asks. "Is there any reason you can think of that he'd leave that message on a photo from the races that day?"

"I don't know. He used to say that to me... Be good for Renni." I close my eyes, letting the memory come back to me. "She lived in this big high-rise on Lex and Fifty-Ninth, right near the six train. He'd bring me up to her apartment for the session, but it was kind of like therapy—he wouldn't come in with me. He'd wait for me in the lobby of her building until the time was up. But now that I'm thinking about it... That's the weird thing."

"How so?"

I open my eyes and meet his gaze. "He'd come up at the end of the session, only to tell us he had an errand to run. That's when he'd say it to me—be good for Renni. Then he'd leave me with her for like fifteen or twenty minutes, and we'd just keep hanging out, drinking tea, practicing Tarot. He'd come back, pay her, and we'd be off."

"Every time, it was like that?"

I nod. "And I saw her once a week for the longest time. Probably for about three years, maybe more. But that was a couple of years after the day at the racetrack, so I'm not sure why he'd write about her on the photo of Shoot the Messenger."

"What was the errand?"

"I have no idea. He never said."

"Does the key look familiar?" he hands it back to me, and I look it over, my mind churning with possibilities. A hidden locker? A secret cache squirreled away for a rainy day? A hope chest of my mother's witchy stuff?

"I've never seen it before," I say. "Not that I remember. But this feels important, Rook. There's something to this. I'm sure of it. And Shoot the Messenger showed up in my nightmare. That has to mean... I don't know." I laugh. "But it's right there in his name—Messenger. I'm totally taking that as a sign."

Rook beams at me, his honey eyes shining. "You are a regular little Sherlock Holmes, aren't you?"

I stretch up on my toes and loop my arms around his neck, and he strokes a massive gargoyle hand down my back, unleashing a soft sigh, our horse-and-key mystery momentarily forgotten.

"I'm learning from the best, professor peepshow," I tease.

Rook laughs, but he doesn't release me. Just keeps stroking me up and down, his claws scraping gently. "Is that a thing now? We're making that a thing?"

"Just between us. Besides, you got to watch me do *very* dirty things to Auggie. The least you could do is let me have a few naughty professor fantasies about *you*."

He tightens his arms around me, his cock stirring beneath the loincloth, pressing against my stomach. "You have naughty professor fantasies about me?"

"Sure do. I'm having one right now, actually."

A soft moan rumbles through his chest, his eyes darkening with lust. "Tell me," he whispers. "Tell me what I'm doing to you in your wild little fantasies."

"Well, you... you're kissing me," I whisper, then close my

eyes, a spark of hunger sizzling through me—the same kind of hunger I felt last night. Untamed. Insatiable.

Goddess, I should shut it down before it gets worse, but...

"That's how it starts, anyway," I say. "A kiss. Our first kiss, right here in the library."

"And then what happens?"

I swallow hard, my pussy clenching at the sultry tone of his voice, at the sudden brazenness from my otherwise sweet, reserved, hyper-logical book nerd.

"I don't know," I admit. "I haven't gotten that far yet." I let out a soft laugh. "Truth be told, I think about kissing you a *lot*. Way more than I should."

Heat spreads across his cheeks, darkening his gray skin with a hint of plum. "I think about it too," he admits. "Way more than I should."

"Maybe we should stop thinking about it," I whisper.

He cups my face, lowering his mouth to mine. "Maybe we should."

Butterflies tumble through my stomach, but at the very first brush of those soft, sexy lips against my mouth, the door bangs open, and Auggie barges into the library, his eyes wide.

"Yes, well. Hate to kill the mood when the world's sexiest nerd is *finally* about to bust a move," he says, "but... Seriously. Come with me, now. There's something you guys need to see."

CHAPTER TWENTY-NINE

AUGUSTINE

The red light of the darkroom soothes my soul, the scent of the developing chemicals as familiar to me as the scent of old books is to Rook or fresh blood is to Jude.

It's a bit crowded with three of us in here—I'm used to working alone—but I'm happy for the company.

It's one more thing West has brought me—a reminder of how important my brothers are to me, and a need to be closer to them. Like a real family—a family we all started taking for granted after so many centuries together. And now Westlyn herself is part of that family—the beautiful, courageous witch we'd all die to protect.

It's that instinctual urge to protect her that has me calling them closer now, the three of us huddling around the photos I've hung from a thin rope stretching from one side of the small space to the other.

The runes West carved on the bodies glow bright

against their skin, the images grotesque in the red light. But that's not what I need them to see.

"Look." I point to the three photos closest to us—enlargements from the series I shot while West was slicing and dicing. They're not entirely in focus—I was too shocked by what was happening to properly frame the shots—but you can see West in each one of them. Her back is to the camera, her hair tied up, giving us a clear view of the back of her neck.

And the dark fae rune glowing there, just beneath her hairline.

"What the fuck?" She touches the spot on one of the photos, her other hand scratching the back of her neck. "I don't have a mark there, do I?"

"It's not visible now, no," I confirm.

"So it's probably just dust on your lens or something, right?" Rook asks.

"I wish it was." I point it out in other photos—at least a dozen of West, all showing the same mark in the same position on her neck. "If that was dust or a crack in the lens, or even a lens flare, it wouldn't show up like this, always in the same spot on West's skin."

"But... I don't understand." West turns to me, her eyes searching mine in the dim red light. "Did you guys notice it last night? What about when you were behind me, when we... Come on, Auggie. You were *right* there. You would've seen it."

"I know. And it's not like I don't pay attention to every

inch of you, witchling." I smile and cup her face between my hands, but I can't hide the concern in my voice. "I don't know why the lens picked it up when we couldn't see it. I'll take some more photos of you tonight, if you're okay with that. See if it shows up again."

She nods and blows out a breath, but her eyes are frantic with fear. "What the hell do you think it is?"

"It appears to be some sort of binding rune." Rook adjusts his glasses and brings in one of the prints for a closer look. "I'll need to do more research to confirm, but I'm almost positive that's what we're looking at."

"Why would I have a dark fae binding rune on my neck?" She rubs her skin as if she can make it disappear. "What does it do?"

"In most cases," he says, "binding runes are used to contain power—kind of like a magical lockbox."

"Most cases? What are the others?"

"Sometimes they can be used to siphon power from one person or object to another, as with a curse. Our gargoyle curse, for example, is bound by demonic magic. It makes the dark fae part of the spell that much more terrible and powerful."

"But I *have* no magic. I was born impotent."

"Unless you weren't," I say. "What if you *weren't* born without magic, West? What if that magic was just... just bound?"

"Eloise," she whispers, tears filling her eyes. "What if she—"

"Hey." Rook draws her into his embrace, rubbing slow circles on her back. "For one thing, Eloise isn't fae, and this is definitely a fae rune. More importantly, we said we wouldn't jump to conclusions, right? This is another clue. Another piece of the puzzle. You've been marked with a fae rune—it appears to be a binding rune. We don't know why, or by whom, or when."

"If it showed up last night," she says, "maybe I caused it. Whatever happened to me when I was cutting up those mages... I didn't feel like myself. I still can't remember it. Maybe I—"

"Correlation does not imply causation." Rook pulls back, his hands wrapped around her arms. "It's possible the two things *are* related, but we can't say for sure your actions last night caused the rune to appear, any more than we can say the rune caused your actions last night. We have to—"

"Do more research," she says with a soft sigh. "I'm catching on."

Rook smiles. "You really are a quick study."

"Told you."

"Auggie," he says, "anything else from the photos? Did you notice any other inconsistencies?"

"Not yet, but I've got a few more rolls to develop from earlier in the night. Rook, the runes... the way they glowed like that on the bodies... It reminded me of moonlight."

He nods. "It probably *is*. Dark fae... they're able to manipulate moonlight for their spells—to use it as a sort of magical ink. It's part of what makes them so powerful."

West touches the back of her neck again, her face pale. "The verse," she whispers. "I heard it with my Tarot reading."

She recites the words for us:

> *Upon those screaming hours*
> *Bathed in blood and breath*
> *You will give them light, my moon*
> *And I will give them Death.*

"My moon? What if that's what the message was referring too—these moonlight runes? I made them—I gave them light."

"If that's what the message meant," Rook says gently, "Then we'll add it to the rest of the puzzle pieces and come up with a plan for what to do next. Okay?"

West nods, but doesn't say anything in response. Just paces along the row of photos strung up on the line, her eyes wide, as if she still can't believe she's responsible for all that carnage.

I want to tell her that they deserved it. That they got off easy after what they did to her. That Jude and I would've *gladly* prolonged their suffering.

But I know it won't help. Looking at the photos, coming face-to-face with her violent actions in stark snapshots, each moment frozen in time... Whether West remembers committing that violence or not, it happened. And realizing that you're capable of something so destructive, so heinous? *That's* the most terrifying part of all.

Jude was right last night—if West had actually killed them, it would've destroyed some precious part of her she'd never get back.

Unfortunately, looking at her now, I'm pretty sure she lost some part of herself anyway.

"Hey," I say softly, nodding toward the exit. "I can finish this up later. Why don't we go see what kind of trouble we can get into in the kitchen? I'm pretty sure there's a vegan nacho recipe with your name all over it."

No response.

"Homemade salsa, hand-smashed guacamole, all your favorite vegetables sautéed to golden perfection..." I laugh, knowing I'm laying it on a bit thick, but desperate to distract her anyway. To bring the light back into her eyes, the sweet smile to her face. "Hey, I'll even throw in some extra tortilla chips for Huxley and Lucinda."

She finally—finally looks at me again, a faint smile touching her lips. "You drive a hard bargain, Auggie."

"Listen. When it comes to nachos, I don't mess around."

With one final glance at the images, she finally allows me to usher her out of the darkroom. Behind me, Rook removes the photos from the line, assembling them into a neat stack.

"You coming with us?" I ask. "You can regale us with tales about the history of guacamole. I'm sure you know it."

Rook laughs, but it dies out fast. "You guys go ahead. I'd

like to get a jump on translating some of these runes, if you don't mind." He points to one of the photos of the rune on West's neck. Then, dropping his voice to a whisper only I can hear, "I've got a bad feeling about this one, Augs. *Real* bad."

CHAPTER THIRTY

WESTLYN

"No... no! I didn't *do* this! I'm not—"

"Open your eyes," a new voice says, deep and smooth, right at the edge of my awareness. "Just a bad dream, love."

"Help me! Somebody help!"

"Wake up," he says softly. A warm hand rubs my back, his touch as comforting as his voice, like soft waves nipping at bare summer toes. "Wake up, Miss Avery. Open your eyes, love..."

"No!" I jolt awake with a gasp, awareness slamming back into me from all sides.

Another fucking nightmare.

I'm lying in Jude's bed—naked, per his request, the sheet clutched to my chest, my heart pounding. My bare back is exposed to the gargoyle currently tracing gentle circles down my spine with the tips of his claws.

Goddess, that feels so good...

"Jude," I breathe, smiling as I turn to face him.

"No, love," he says. "It's me, I'm afraid."

It takes a moment for my eyes to adjust in the darkness. "Draegan?"

Draegan jerks back abruptly—a kid caught with a hand in the cookie jar.

"What are you doing in here?" I hiss, then immediately regret it.

Shit. I didn't mean to sound so harsh, but... I'm naked. In Jude's bed. And Draegan is sitting on the edge of it as if my skin suddenly burned him, and now he's just staring mutely at my...

Awesome.

Hello, boobs. I see we're just hanging out there now, bobbing around for all the world to see!

I yank the sheet up to my neck and glare at him, but do you think the broody beast will actually *admit* he's acting like a grade-A weirdo? Ha! I've got a better chance of sprouting wings and a tail and declaring *myself* a gargoyle.

"Considering this is my home, Miss Avery," he snaps, folding his arms across his chest and turning his nose up in the air, "I'm free to enter any room as I see fit. Perhaps I should be asking *you* the questions."

I didn't see him at all last night—haven't seen him once since he carried me up to his bed after what shall forever be known as the Night of a Thousand Finger-Bangs, and *this* is what he's leading with? Attitude and evasion?

Still clutching the sheet to my chest, I sit up and make a

show of bowing my head. You know, to really send the message home. "Oh, by all means, your *lordship*. Ask away. I live to serve you, especially when you wake me out of a dead sleep for no other reason than to harass me."

He scoffs at me, but his anger fades quickly, his eyes filling with concern and—if I'm not mistaken—tenderness.

That, more than anything, sets off my alarms.

"What is it?" I ask, dropping the snark. "What's wrong? Is it Jude? Did he find Metal and—"

"Jude's fine." He turns away from me to give me a bit of privacy, his wings slumping. "We *did* find Nesterman—at home in Bayside with his girlfriend. A witch by the name of Kelly."

I swallow hard. "Did Jude…"

I don't need to finish the sentence.

"Oh, he wanted to. Took some monumental threats on my part to keep him from waltzing in there and causing a bloodbath. Can't say I blame him—Nesterman inspires violence in us all."

"So what happens next?"

"We're not sure yet. We're going to discuss it with Rook later—see what other intel he's come up with from those cell phones." Draegan sighs. "Jude promised to behave himself. I just hope he can last another night."

"I'll talk to him."

He nods, then glances at me over his shoulder. "Still having nightmares, then?"

"Unfortunately, yes." I press a hand to my chest. My

heart is still slamming against my ribs, the last of Zorakkov's tendrils not quite ready to recede from my mind.

"It would seem your 'nocturnal reframing' efforts aren't going so well," he teases, finally getting a smile out of me.

"About as well as your attempts to dodge my earlier question." I nudge his thigh with my foot. "So, you gonna level with me about why you're skulking around the bedroom while I sleep like some kind of... well, like Jude?"

Draegan lets out a quiet laugh, but it's quickly overtaken by a deep sigh. "Augustine told me about the mark."

"The... oh. Right." That explains why he was touching my back—just wanted to see if he could find the mark, is all. Nothing more, nothing less.

That probably shouldn't disappoint me as much as it does, but...

Sigh.

Wrapping the sheet around me like a toga, I rise from the bed and go stand near the window, gathering my hair and lifting it off my nape. "Do you see anything in the moonlight? I was trying to look earlier with a mirror, but I couldn't find it."

He joins me at the window. Close. Too close. The heat from his body envelopes me, his breath misting against my bare skin as he leans in to examine the mark.

His touch is powder-soft, fingers spanning the base of my neck, their gentle touch sending a shower of sparks skittering down my spine.

It triggers something in me, that touch. His breath. His nearness and the scent of his skin, like a storm-tossed sea that promises only death to anyone who dares to get close.

I suck in a breath, remembering the mages on their knees.

Remembering the blood as Jude made the death cuts.

Remembering how I begged Auggie... and the feel of him inside me—his tail, his tongue.

And after, the desperate need I felt in the car when I begged Draegan to touch me and he made me feel so...

I gasp, and Draegan lowers his hand and takes a step back.

There's no hiding his effect on me, all of it magnified by a million since the other night.

He may as well be reading my mind.

Blowing out a shaky breath, I plaster on a smile and turn to face him again, ignoring the burning need between my thighs and forcing the memories of his perfect fingers out of my mind.

Pay rent, or get the fuck out, assholes...

"Anything?" I ask.

He arcs a sexy eyebrow over a slate-gray eye, and I swear I see a flicker of desire there. The air between us crackles with electric heat, with wanting, with all the unnamed things that have been swirling between us since the very first moments in the bell tower...

But before either of us can make a move to tear down the walls and just... just *do* something about it, he turns away. Crosses the room, moving about as far from me as he can get.

"No," he says firmly, and I'm not sure whether he means no, he doesn't see the mark, or no, we can't acknowledge this thing between us, let alone act on it.

Whatever the hell it even is.

"Draegan, I—"

"Have you always had it?" He wraps his hand around the back of his neck, rubbing the spot where the mark supposedly lives on mine. "Since childhood, even?"

So we're back to the mark, then. Ooh-kay...

"Maybe? For all I know, I could've been born with it—it's not like my father would've said anything. He had a hard enough time trying to convince people I wasn't a total freak." I sigh and lean back against the window, the glass cold on my bare shoulders.

Across the moonlit room, Draegan's eyes are dark and intense. Impossible to read, as usual.

"Draegan," I whisper, another terrifying idea taking root. "What if... what if the dark fae... I don't know. Put some kind of claim on me? What if it's not just Zorakkov and the shadow magic society coming for me, but the fae, too?"

CHAPTER THIRTY-ONE

WESTLYN

"Not a fucking *chance*." Draegan's claws burst free, and he crosses the room in three long strides, stopping just before me. With the lightest touch of a claw beneath my chin, he tilts my face up, his voice a deadly whisper. "You are *ours*, Westlyn Avery. I told you that from the start. We're not going to let anyone—or any *thing*—take you from us. Not some demon prince. Not the Archmage and his minions. Not the fucking dark fae. *No* one. *That* is a promise you can take to the fucking bank."

Fury flashes through his eyes, vibrates through his chest and arms, yet still his touch remains gentle. Gentle as he moves from my chin and traces that same claw along my jaw. Gentle as he cups my cheek. Gentle as he lowers his mouth to mine.

But then, all too soon, he's closing his eyes and

muttering a curse. Releasing me. Turning his back and walking toward the door.

Confusing and frustrating me yet again.

"Wait! I mean... Take it to the bank?" I force out a laugh, if only to make him turn around and look at me with the ocean in his eyes again. To make him stay, just a little longer. "No one goes to the bank anymore."

"For fuck's sake, little mortal. Sometimes I forget how young you really are." He finally turns around, an actual smile gracing his grim face, vanquishing some of the weirdness between us. Running a hand through his salt-and-pepper hair, he says, "It's an old idiom that basically means you can absolutely count on whatever's being said, just like you can redeem a bank check at face value."

"No, I get that. I just think it's a *weird* idiom, is all. People do most of their banking on apps or online these days. Idioms should be updated for modern usage so that the shared meaning isn't lost."

Another smile. A sparkle in his eyes rather than darkness, rather than fury. "Channeling Rook, are we?"

"He'd totally have my back on this. You can take *that* to the bank."

"I'm sure he—"

"Wait!" I gasp, the realization hitting me hard. "Draegan. That's it! The bank!"

"Are we... still talking about idioms?"

"My father left something for me at the bank!" In a frantic, fevered rush, I tell him about Shoot the Messenger and the mysterious note on the photo. The key. Renni. My father's random errands. "I told Rook my father never said what the errands were, but now I remember—he *did* say something. Right before he left, he'd say, 'I have to take something to the bank.'"

"Every time?"

"Yes! Goddess, it's coming back to me now. Her building was right next to the Bank of New Amsterdam's main branch. That's where he'd go. And he always made a point of telling me, too. He'd put his hand on my shoulders, look me in the eyes, and say, 'Be good for Renni. I have to take something to the bank. Do you understand?' I always thought it was weird how he was so adamant about it. Like, I remember thinking, um... okay? Go to the bank, then."

"Miss Avery, I'm still not sure what you're getting at here."

"The key, Draegan," I say, pacing as a flood of nervous energy zips through my veins. "It was taped inside the frame of one of the only photos I have of the two of us together—me, my dad, and the horse, Shoot the Messenger. A losing horse he bet on time and again, leaving the ticket stubs around the brownstone for me to find, just so I'd subconsciously realize the importance of that photo. No, not the horse. Not some special moment we shared. The key! It was always about the key. Then he wrote that random note about Renni—a witch healer we didn't even keep in touch with—all so I'd make the connection about the bank, which I only made because he said it so many times like a freaking robot. There's no other explanation." I stop pacing and turn to look at him again, my heart thundering, my words coming faster than I can even process them.

Draegan looks like his head is about to explode. Forcing myself to slow down, I say, "Draegan, that key belongs to a safe deposit box at the Bank of New Amsterdam, and my father left something for me there. I'm positive."

He considers me a few moments, still trying to piece together my mile-a-minute ramble, then says, "All right, then. If it's a safe deposit box key, and the box is located in that bank, perhaps we could—"

"It *is*," I insist. "I can feel it. But..." My heart sinks. "What am I saying? I can't exactly walk in there like, 'Hey! I'm Westlyn Avery! I'm pretty sure my deadbeat dad left me some sort of clue about my whole witch-fae-demon-bride destiny before he skipped town with my evil stepmother, never to be heard from again. I don't know the box number or anything, and I'm not even sure it's listed under his real name, but could you maybe just break *every* single one of your security protocols and allow me to—"

Draegan presses a clawed finger to my lips, new mirth dancing in his eyes. "As much as I enjoy your legendary rants, I might actually know someone who can help."

I roll my eyes, and he removes his claw from my lips.

"Who?" I snark. "The bank president?"

"Vice president, actually, but he'll do. Kevin Klaiburn,

he's called. A longtime associate of the men of shadow and stone."

"You're... serious? Wow. You've got a bank VP in your back pocket, just hanging around waiting to break the rules for you?" I laugh, because, of *course* he does.

Draegan shrugs. "*Bend* the rules, more like. It's not as if we're trying to commit a heist."

"No, but whatever we need to do to get into that box is probably illegal. Why would he stick his neck out like that?"

"In addition to serving as the bank's VP, Klaiburn also owns a number of high-end underground sex clubs throughout the city. That in itself is rather unremarkable, but—"

I laugh. "That's unremarkable? I can't wait to hear the remarkable part, then."

"He's embezzling client funds from the bank to cover his operating expenses at the clubs. It's not always profitable."

"Wow. Okay. And you've got proof of this, I assume?"

"Oh, yes. Rook has a whole dossier. Profit and loss statements, pie charts, lists of all the clubs' members and guests—very high-profile individuals. The sort of people who would not want their names being leaked to the press after Klaiburn promised them absolute privacy at all costs."

"You guys are scary. Like, legit scary."

He leans in close, his breath tickling my ear. "Good thing we're on your side, then."

"My thoughts exactly. I'm—"

"Well, *this* is unexpected." Jude saunters into the room, his smile mischievous. "Cozy, too. It's not often you pay a visit to my room, Draegan. To what do I owe the honor?"

"Miss Avery and I were just... having a discussion."

Jude leans in and kisses my cheek. Then my mouth. Then his hand starts tugging my sheet down—

"Jude!" I slap him and pull away. "Draegan is standing right there!"

"Oh, I don't think he minds a bit." Jude winks at me and turns to look at Draegan. In a low, sultry voice that has me instantly wet, he says, "Westlyn and I need to have a... *non*-discussion. You're welcome to join us, if you'd like—that is, if the little scarecrow doesn't mind?"

Jude presses a kiss to the hollow of my throat. Then lower. Across my collarbone, back to my throat, slowly dragging his mouth down, down, down...

My gaze involuntarily slides to Draegan's. His eyes smolder, his jaw set tight.

That now-familiar hunger burns through me anew, my nipples aching, nerves sizzling, every muscle wound tight and ready to unleash.

I'm just about to open my big dumb mouth—*Mind? Not at all! Please make yourself at home between my thighs! Both of you! At the same time!*—when Draegan closes his eyes, shutting down the brief connection between us.

"You've got ninety minutes, Miss Avery," he says, all business once again, then turns on his heel and heads for the door.

"Ninety minutes for what?"

"To wrap up your non-discussion with Jude, shower, find some clothing—something inconspicuous this time, if you don't mind—and meet me in the garage." He looks over his shoulder at me and flashes one last devastating grin. "You and I are going on another road trip."

CHAPTER THIRTY-TWO

DRAEGAN

Keeping her tucked in close, I escort Westlyn through Blackmoor Capital's underground parking garage and into our private elevator, zooming us up to the executive floor. It's composed entirely of our offices, though the others don't spend much time here. Especially now that Westlyn has taken up residence at the manor—they prefer to be there with her. With each other.

Frankly, I'd like nothing more than to be there with them. But we can't afford to let our other duties fall by the wayside. Westlyn is absolutely the priority, but while I'm working to keep tabs on the stone gargoyles of this city, and juggling the endless investigations and meetings and bribes that keep our organization running as smoothly as it can, I just have to trust the others to protect her.

I don't always agree with their methods—*Looking at* you,

Jude—but I do know they'll do anything in their power to keep her safe.

Tonight, though? She's all mine.

"Just through here, love," I say, escorting her through the glass doors of the reception area, then down the hall to a massive oak door at the end.

She enters ahead of me, slowly turning on her heel to take it all in—the midnight blue walls, the hardwood floors, the massive bookcases, a huge mahogany desk and conference table, and—its most impressive feature—the bank of floor-to-ceiling windows spanning the far wall, granting us a view of the city lights beyond. "Whoa. This is your office?"

"The primary one, yes."

"No wonder you spend so much time here. Did you decorate all this yourself?"

"I designed the interior layout, and I selected all the colors, finishes, and furniture. But people far more skilled than I put it all together."

"I've never seen anything like it. It's gorgeous. Incredible—like something out of your magazines." She turns to me and smiles, her eyes glittering.

Warmth spirals through my chest.

"I'm glad you approve." I close the door behind us and drop my human glamour, pleased to see my assistant has already set up the conference table with the takeaway I requested. "Let me take your coat."

She removes the conservative dark gray trench coat and hands it over, revealing...

For fuck's sake, Westlyn Avery. It's possible you've found a way to send an immortal to his grave.

I take in the outfit, head to toe. Thigh-high black leather boots that are already giving me *very* bad ideas. A black leather skirt that laces up the sides, entirely inappropriate for the office. Some sort of strappy black leather-and-metal halter top that leaves very little to the imagination and is somehow even *less* appropriate than the skirt.

"Draegan? You still with me?" She waves a hand in front of my face, her eyes bright. "You zoned out for a minute there."

"Miss Avery, when I said to wear something inconspicuous tonight..." I clear my throat, trying like hell to keep my eyes on hers and not on all that smooth, bared skin. "It seems something was lost in translation."

"It's New York City! This is *totally* inconspicuous. Besides, Jude ordered me a bunch of new clothes. I wanted to try them out." She laughs, flipping her long hair over her shoulder. "And if you think the *outfit* is extra, you should see the bras and panties he—"

I hold up a hand, cutting her off before my heart bloody stops.

"Have a seat at the table. I'll be right with you." I force a polite smile, then bury myself in the closet, taking my time hanging up her coat. Of all the negotiations I thought I'd be engaging in tonight, trying to convince my cock to settle down was *not* one of them.

"What's all this?" Westlyn asks when I finally join her at the table.

"I've only just sent word to Mr. Klaiburn—we've got some time before he arrives. I figured you might be hungry, so I had my assistant order in for us."

"Wait. You... have an assistant?"

"Oh, yes. He's worked for us for years. Joshua Barrons, he goes by now, though I'm not sure what his original name is. It's impolite to ask."

"I take it he's not human?"

"Fae. We don't have many employees at Blackmoor—we prefer to handle most things ourselves, and we use subcontractors for the few tasks we can't or don't want to deal with. As for the rest, we've adopted a *strict* no-humans policy. Given the nature of our work, we can't risk the potential exposure."

"Is he still here? Can I meet him?"

"No." I pull out one of the leather executive chairs and gesture for her to take a seat. "Like any good employee, Joshua knows the fine art of making himself constantly available, yet entirely unseen."

Westlyn doesn't take her seat. She just stares at the food, absently chewing on her thumbnail.

"Far be it from me to criticize your sophisticated palate," I tease, "but I'm almost certain the takeaway is better than your thumbnail."

She lowers her hand and smiles, but doesn't make a

move to sit. "Thanks, but I think I'm too nervous to sit, let alone eat."

"Miss Avery. I'm quite certain you haven't eaten tonight."

She laughs. "How could you possibly know that?"

"Before we left Blackmoor, you spent the first hour of your evening engaged in a thorough... ahem... non-discussion with Jude, followed by a shower and entirely too much time getting dressed, considering what little clothing you're actually wearing. There was also an unscheduled wandering of the orchard with Lucinda and Huxley... I very nearly left you there."

"I wasn't *wandering*." She heads over to the massive windows, gazing out across the city. "Jean-Pierre was in town. We were catching up."

"Catching up?"

"He's not as comfortable around new people as his siblings, so he's been keeping a low profile. He brought me this, though." She turns toward me again, fingering the jeweled hairpin fastened above her ear. "He's thoughtful like that."

"I'm sure he is." I try not to sigh. "You still haven't mentioned eating anything."

"I had a latte."

Leaving her chair pulled out, I take a seat at the head of the table, shaking out a cloth napkin and placing it in my lap. "You're a human girl, and you need to eat real food. You can't subsist on caffeine and sugar."

"Wanna bet?" she laughs.

I glare at her across the table, my blood simmering. Fifteen-hundred odd years alive, and no one has ever, *ever* been able to push my buttons so thoroughly as this infuriating woman.

"No. Sit down."

"I told you, I'm not hungry and—"

"And *I'm* not interested in indulging childish antics tonight. So you can either sit in your chair like a good girl and feed yourself, or sit on my lap while I do it for you." I flash a menacing grin, the warning in my voice clear. "Guess which option will be more pleasant?"

Fuck.

It's the wrong card to play. I know it the moment the words are out. The light in her eyes darkens, and she squares her shoulders, her lips quirking at the corners.

"Miss *Avery*," I warn, but it's too late. She's already stalking toward me. Swiveling my chair around. And dropping herself right into my lap, intentionally grinding that hot little arse against my cock.

I should've seen it coming, but I didn't. As usual, the incorrigible little witch knows *exactly* what she's doing, and despite my best efforts, I've let her get the upper hand.

Again.

"Yay!" She claps with mock exuberance, still wiggling, still determined to completely *destroy* me. "What's on the menu? Smells delish, but I hope it's vegan. Also, have you reviewed my most up-to-date list of food allergies? It's quite extensive. You wouldn't want me to go into anaphylactic shock just to prove a point, would you?"

"I'm well aware of your dietary needs. The food is from a famous vegan restaurant nearby that also happens to be one of the few restaurants in this city that meets Augustine's impossibly high culinary standards and for fuck's *sake*, Miss Avery, will you *please* stop wiggling?"

"Wiggling? This?" She does it again. "This is merely adjusting. Repositioning. Wiggling is more like…"

She shimmies in my lap, her skirt riding up until there's barely anything between us but my loincloth and the napkin. Oh, and those panties Jude dressed her in, no doubt.

"*Westlyn*," I grind out. "Stop… stop moving. For the love of all that is sacred, stop *bloody* moving."

I'm already rock hard for her, my cock throbbing against her tight arse, her body warm and perfect and fucking *hell* it's all I can do to hold on to the last threads of my control…

"And what if I don't?" She shifts again, smug and defiant as ever. "Are you finally going to make good on all your threats, or—*shit!*"

In a flash I've got her flipped over and sprawled out across my lap, her arms flailing, skirt pushed up, her ripe arse in full view—twin pale orbs contained behind a purple lace thong, all that flesh just *begging* for my handprint.

"Draegan!" she squeals. "What the hell are you doing?"

"You still haven't learned your lesson about taunting me,

little mortal." I graze my palm across her smooth skin, enjoying the ripple of gooseflesh that follows. "That's quite... unfortunate."

"Put me down!"

"Hmm. Is that really what you want?"

She doesn't answer. Just wrenches out of my grasp and gets to her feet, her cheeks red, hair falling in front of her eyes.

The scent of her desire... *Fuck.*

"Seriously?" she hisses, pushing her hair back and straightening her skirt, doing her damndest to appear angry. "You were *seriously* going to spank me?"

I shrug. "You need a lesson in manners and discipline."

"Oh, really? And you think you're the one to teach me?" Heat flares in her eyes—a challenge brewing. Then, dropping her voice to a seductive whisper that only portends my doom, "Be my guest, *Daddy Drae*."

CHAPTER THIRTY-THREE

DRAEGAN

Fuck.

Those words. That whisper. Those fucking boots and the purple lace thong and that smart little mouth and...

I rise from the chair to my full height, wings unfurling, claws bursting free. She backs up toward my desk, bumping into the chair behind it and letting out a little yelp.

Glaring down at her startled turquoise eyes, I say darkly, "Take off everything but the boots and panties and get on your knees, Miss Avery."

She crosses her arms over her chest and cocks an eyebrow, but we've come too far in our little game to back down now.

In a low growl, I make the demand once more. "On. Your. *Knees.*"

Fire flickers through her gaze and I wait for her to call

my bluff. To tell me to fuck off in all the cute and clever ways I know she wants to.

But the little mortal merely lowers her arms.

Grins.

Removes the leather halter top. Steps out of the skirt. Stands before me in her lacy-thonged, black-booted glory...

And then drops to her knees.

Fuck. Me.

Her dark pink nipples stand at attention, each one begging to be sucked.

I still haven't been able to rid my mind of the memories from our drive home the other night, try as I might. I've mostly avoided her since, not wanting to blur the lines any more than I already have.

It's too risky. Dangerous, especially now that we're dealing with dark fae runes and memory loss and whatever else we've yet to uncover about the vast mysteries of Westlyn Avery.

About her connection to us, to our curse.

Logically, I know I should walk away. Every cell in my body is screaming at me to do the honorable thing. The responsible thing. The *right* thing.

But as she gazes up at me through those dark lashes, her eyes daring me to cross yet another line between us, her tongue darting out to moisten those lush, red lips, my mouth already watering for a taste of those tits, all sense of honor and responsibility and rightness vanish.

I cup her face, sliding a thumb across her lower lip as I

free my aching cock from beneath the loincloth. It's rock-hard for her and hot to the touch, pre-cum beading at the tip.

"Are you going to suck it for me?" I whisper, sliding the tip across those painted red lips. "That's what you want?"

"Please," she whispers, hot breath swirling across my flesh. "Let me taste you, Daddy."

"Take it," I command. "Show Daddy how good you take his cock in your mouth."

She opens wider for me, lips wrapping around the end, her tongue sliding along the underside and—

I go still. The scent of intruders—fae and human both—and two pairs of footsteps linger just outside the door.

In a blur, I've got my glamour back in place and my witch shoved under the desk, hidden from view a mere instant before my door bangs open.

I drop into the chair just as two figures charge through the doorway—Kevin Klaiburn and Joshua Barrons.

"I'm sorry, Draegan," Joshua says, clearly flustered. "The man refused to wait."

Beneath the desk, I press a finger to Westlyn's lips, silently begging her to keep her mouth shut.

Joshua knows I've got a guest tonight, but that's all he was told about the matter.

And Klaiburn?

He doesn't need to know *anything*. Westlyn was supposed to be locked away in my bathroom by the time he got here, well and truly out of sight.

Damn it.

"It's all right, Joshua." I gesture for him to leave, then smile at Klaiburn, my teeth clenched. "Mr. Klaiburn. I wasn't expecting you for another hour."

The old man bristles. "Funny, considering I wasn't expecting to be *expected* at all. Yet here I am, summoned to midtown well after business hours for some emergency your assistant didn't have the decency to explain on the phone."

"Need I remind you—"

He cuts me off with a raised hand. "If I needed a reminder, I wouldn't have come at all. So tell me." He takes a seat in the chair on the other side of my desk. "What is this about?

"I need... oh, *fuck*..."

It's official. Westlyn Avery is a fucking health hazard, not to mention a damn menace. Tucked away beneath the desk, the little brat is toying with me, her hands sliding up my thighs, clever fingers already freeing my cock. I'm in the human glamour, but... bloody hell, the parts still work the same. *Feel* the same as she wraps her hand around me and strokes...

"Pardon me?" Klaiburn narrows his eyes.

"I meant... I need... luck. A bit of luck and a favor from you about..." I grip one of her wrists, but she's already got the other hand on standby, fisting me harder, her lips so close...

She's going to repay me for all the things I said to her tonight. For the near spanking. For putting her on her knees. And there's not a damn thing I can do about it. Not without making her presence known to the banker—an outcome that may not be deadly, but one I'd rather avoid nevertheless.

There was a reason I asked her to dress inconspicuously tonight. A reason I brought her straight from the garage to the elevator. A reason I've got her shoved under the desk now.

I don't know how many shadow magic society members exist in this city. I don't know who's in their pockets, who's under their protection, who's being threatened and willing to throw someone else to the wolves in order to save their own arses.

"Out with it, Caldwell," the man huffs. "I haven't got all night."

Westlyn's tongue skates across the tip of my cock, a ripple of warm, wet pleasure so intense it damn near shatters my glamour.

Fuck... I need to push her away before she gets us both caught.

But she feels too fucking good, too perfect, and at the next stroke of her naughty little tongue, I'm gone.

All I can do is hold on for the ride.

And get this cad out of my office.

"I need access to a safe deposit box at your institution," I blurt out. "Fifty-Ninth and Lexington branch."

"To whom does this box belong?"

"They're..." I close my eyes, trying not to grunt at the pleasure of her incessant licks. "...deceased."

As I'm about to be...

"Of course they are." He huffs out a dark laugh. "Your doing, I presume?"

I say nothing, but not because I didn't understand his question or his meaning.

I say nothing, but not because I'm trying to avoid implicating myself in another murder.

I say nothing, but not out of any desire to intimidate the man with my stone-cold silence.

I say *nothing* because I'm about ten seconds from flipping this fucking desk and spilling down the little mortal's throat, and to be perfectly honest, I'm not even sure I remember how to speak in complete fucking sentences anymore and... oh, bloody *hell* why does her soft little mouth feel like that?

"Mr. Caldwell? Are you quite all right?"

"Yes, I'm just..." I press a fist to my chest, trying to breathe through it. "Heartburn."

"Do you need some water?"

I wave off his concern as she relaxes her throat and takes me in deeper, her tongue rippling with every stroke. A soft moan vibrates through her lips, and in that moment I thank the fucking devil Klaiburn is as old as he is, or he might've heard her.

"The name of the box holder is Brian Avery. I want you to... leave me the bank's key to that box and... and clear the branch of all security and evening employees, yourself included…" I swallow hard, barely holding on, barely breathing, my hand pressed to my chest like that heartburn is *really* doing a number on me. "And… insure the security cameras are inoperative for one hour."

"What? How do you propose I do all that?"

"Tell them there's a… a gas leak, or a water main break, or… I don't know, an accidental release of the guest list from one of your clubs and fucking *hell*, Klaiburn!" I slam a fist down on the desk, mere seconds from exploding in her mouth. "Do I need to spell it out? You're a bank VP! Surely you've got the wits to think of some ruse!"

He blinks at me, totally silent. Then, "Are you sure you're not having a heart attack?"

"No, but I will be if you don't leave here at once and do as I ask."

"You're sweating, Mr. Caldwell. You—"

"That will be *all*, Mr. Klaiburn."

He rises from the chair, his face grim, annoyance pinching his brows. He hates me. They all do. But in the end, they all do what I expect of them. That's just how things work among powerful people with dirty secrets.

"I'll text you as soon as I've located the key and the coast is clear," he says, finally heading for the door.

"See that you do. Oh, and Mr. Klaiburn? Close the door behind you, if you don't mind."

He grumbles something under his breath, then slams the door with gusto.

The moment he's gone, the gargoyle bursts free from the glamour.

She had my whole cock in her mouth, the poor girl, and now that it's back in gargoyle form, it's just too big for her to handle. It slips out, that final stroke of her lips and tongue sending me right over the fucking cliff.

I grip the base and growl her name and unload in a white-hot fury, absolutely *painting* her with it—her throat. Her stomach. Those perfect tits.

Still half under my desk, she gasps and closes her eyes and arches her back and takes it. Every hot stroke. Every drop.

When I finally stop trembling, when my balls finally stop humming, when I finally come back to earth, I suck in a deep breath. Hold it. Count to ten.

Then I haul her up off the floor and set her on the desk, caging her between my arms and leaning in so close, I can see the tiny flecks of gold in her eyes.

She's covered in my release, her lips swollen, her breath wild, and I'm fairly certain I'm not even alive anymore.

"*That*," I say, wrapping a claw-tipped hand around her throat, "was unwise."

CHAPTER THIRTY-FOUR

DRAEGAN

"Oh, *yes*," Westlyn says, her tone dripping with sarcasm. "Really bad call on my part. I can tell you hated every minute of—"

I tighten my grip around her throat, and with a soft, final gasp, the words die on her tongue.

I lean in close, pressing my lips to her temple. A deep, animalistic growl vibrates through my chest—a threat and a promise both. "Such a naughty little mortal. How *ever* shall I punish you now?"

She squirms on the desk and claws at my arm, trying but failing to free herself from my treacherous hold. In a small, breathy voice, she says, "Let me go."

"I think you'd rather I let you *come*. However..." I release her throat and drag my claws down through the mess I left on her skin, smearing it over her breasts and stomach as she trembles beneath my touch—a touch that could very easily turn deadly. "If you'd like to end this now, feel free to use your words."

"You... you don't even *know* my words," she breathes.

"Are you certain?" I ask, sweeping lower with the tips of those deadly claws. "When it comes to the events unfolding under my roof, I know more than you realize. So if you truly wish to call this off..."

"But I..." She closes her eyes, clearly at war with herself. "Please."

"Please *what*, little mortal?"

"Draegan," she says, no more than the barest sigh, her thighs parting as my hand skates lower and lower, my claws retracting, one finger slipping inside her lace panties, then another, until I'm at her entrance again, just like the other night.

My fingers are slick with cum. I push it inside her with a deep, deliberate stroke.

And just like that night, I find her warm and willing, eager, her body molding around my fingers as if we were both created and dropped into this wretched existence for the sole purpose of indulging in such hot, filthy pleasures.

"Please," she whispers again.

I slide my fingers in and out, dripping with her desire, with my release. Her body tightens around every slow, delicious thrust. "Please what, little mortal?"

No response but a soft whimper.

"Nothing to say?" I laugh. "Well, that is *highly* unusual

for such an incorrigible, opinionated, mouthy little girl. Does the sudden silence mean you'd like me to stop?"

She shakes her head adamantly. "Don't stop. Whatever you do, don't stop."

"Then tell me. Tell me *exactly* what my greedy girl wants."

"I... I want you to make me come."

My cock is already stirring again at her words. At her scent.

I brush my lips across her mouth, smearing what's left of her red lipstick. In a dark, dangerous whisper, I say, *"Beg me for it."*

There's no resistance. No arguing. No button pushing.

"Please," she whimpers. "I'm begging you, Draegan. I'll... I'll do whatever you want. Eat the food, stop mouthing off, let you bend me over your knee and—goddess, just please, please, *please* make me come."

"Hmm. So selfish," I taunt with a low chuckle. "You may be accustomed to batting those lashes and getting your way with the others, but after that stunt you just pulled under the desk, I'm not giving you another *inch* tonight, little mortal. If there's something more you desire from me, you're going to have to bloody well *take* it."

I draw back from her wet heat and sit in my desk chair, steepling my hands in my lap, my eyes never leaving hers.

It's another battle of wills, this time to see which of us will move first. I'm the one who backed off, but my skin is already mourning the loss of contact, every muscle in my body twitching with the need to go to her. To fist her hair and tear off those lace panties and fucking *bury* myself in that hot, wet pussy...

"I can't believe I'm about to do this," she says, still breathless, "but... *Damn* it."

She hops off the desk and crosses the short distance to my chair, stopping when my knees bracket her bare thighs.

Keeping my hands firmly locked in place, I say, "Is there something I can help you with, Miss Avery?"

She whimpers again, equal parts need and frustration, my cum still dripping down her chest.

I don't bother trying to hide her effect on me.

But I *am* going to make her work for it. All night long, if I must.

The little brat thinks she can beat me at my own game? We'll see about that.

"Make me come, Daddy," she whispers. "You're so, so good at it. Please."

My cock twitches beneath the loincloth.

Well, *fuck*. So much for my firm stance about the long game.

"Lose the panties," I command. "Now."

I can practically read the string of insults flitting across her eyes, but she doesn't utter a word. She can't—she's too wound up, too desperate for my touch.

Whatever new lines we're about to cross tonight... Perhaps she'll hate herself for this later. Perhaps we'll *both* hate ourselves.

But right now, she'll take exactly what she wants.

And I'll give it to her, no question.

She finally obeys, stepping out of the panties and dangling them from her fingertip. A soft blush stains her cheeks, her black-and-silver hair wild, lips smeared red, those fucking boots already earning a place of honor among my eternal fantasies.

I whip the purple lace out of her hand and press it to my mouth, inhaling her scent, memorizing it.

Growling for it.

"Come. *Here*," I grind out.

Again, she obeys, crawling into my lap and hovering over my cock, my loincloth the only thing between us, and bloody hell I know how badly she wants it. How badly I want it, my cock buried so deep in that soft pussy it will hit the back of her fucking throat.

But this isn't about what either of us wants.

It's about what the little brat *needs*.

"Are you... are you going to touch me?" she whispers, delicate hands curled around my shoulders, cum still running down her chest.

"I told you, little mortal," I say softly. "I'm giving you nothing. If there's something you want, go ahead and *take* it."

Eyes blazing, her small fingers encircle my wrist, and I don't resist as she drags my hand between her thighs, parting to give me better access.

Warmth pulses across my skin, and I straighten my

fingers just outside her entrance, waiting to see what she'll do next.

She looks at me again, pausing as if waiting for permission.

I nod.

She pushes my fingers deep inside her, then drags them out.

"Is this what you want?" I whisper, helping her out with another deep thrust. "To fuck Daddy's hand?"

"Yes. Goddess, yes." She grinds down harder, urging me in deeper.

"That's it. Fuck my fingers, little mortal. Show Daddy what a filthy girl you are."

She releases my wrist and grips my shoulders, grinding down against my palm, angling her body so the heel of my hand rubs her clit, my fingers still pumping slowly inside her. It's not long before she finds her perfect rhythm, writhing in my lap, taking me deeper, gasping with every thrust.

The blush from her cheeks spreads down her neck, her chest, across both breasts. Her black-and-silver hair fans out across them, dark nipples peeking through.

I drag my tongue across one, then the other, making her shudder.

Fuck, her skin is so soft. So perfect.

"More," she whispers. "You feel..." Her eyes are half-lidded as she sinks deeper and deeper into her pleasure, losing herself.

"No." With my free hand, I grip her jaw. "Your eyes are *mine*, Miss Avery. I want them open. I want you *watching* me while you're fucking my hand. I want to see the light dancing in your eyes when you come all over my fingers."

A soft whimper, another roll of her hips, and she finally opens those gorgeous eyes for me again.

But then, just when I'm certain I've got her right where I want her—just when I'm certain I've won this final battle of wills between us—she says, "But I don't want to come on your fingers, Daddy. I want to come on your cock."

Bloody.

Fucking.

Hell.

I'm done. I'm fucking gone. She wins. Hands down, she wins.

Because after *that* little declaration?

Nothing is going to come between my aching cock and her pretty little pussy until I've damn well had my fill and she's in tears from the sheer pleasure of it.

I yank my fingers out of her and grab her by the throat, hauling her close and dragging my mouth across her lips once more.

In a dark whisper, I say, "Do you know what you're getting yourself into with me, little mortal?"

She nods. "Please, Daddy."

I don't give her a chance to say more. With one arm around her waist, I lift her and turn her around, bending her face-forward over my desk.

I skim my palm down her spine, down past the scars carved into her lower back.

I skim my palm back up and fist her hair, knuckles brushing the spot where the fae rune glowed so brightly in Augustine's photos.

"You are a *beautiful* creature, head to toe," I whisper. "But this? This is my *favorite* spot." I bend over her, lifting her hair and buzzing my lips along the back of her neck, suddenly feeling very possessive of that soft skin. "Every time you walk into the room with your hair in one of your messy buns, I watch you. Imagine touching you here. *Licking* you."

I kiss her again, then lick, the tip of my tongue tracing a path from one side to the other, then down. I kiss her shoulder, then slowly move to the other, my fangs grazing her skin, her blood scented with a mix of fear and lust that has me falling even more deeply under her spell.

"Grab the edge of the desk," I tell her, and she obeys at once. I rise to my full height again, freeing my cock and dragging it through her wet heat, one hand still fisting her hair. "Daddy's going to make you come on his cock, little mortal, just like you wanted. But I'm going to come again, too. I'm going to fill this pretty pussy until you can't take another *drop* of me. Understand?"

"Yes."

"Yes, what?"

"Yes, Daddy," she whispers.

Fuck, I'll never get enough of that word, her soft sighs, her bare skin.

"Open wider and lift your hips for me, love," I say, and she does, spreading her legs and arching that lovely backside toward me.

My tail slides around the front, the tip gliding across her clit. She gasps at the contact, and in that breathless moment, I bury my cock deep inside her.

"Draegan," she breathes, her body pulsing around me, the fucking stars dancing behind my eyes, because this?

This...

Fuck.

I stop moving, stop breathing, even try to stop my heartbeat, all of it just so I can freeze this moment in time, sear it right into my brain. If an eternity trapped in stone is my fate, I will *gladly* take this memory with me and forsake all others that came before it as well as all that will come after.

Because bloody *hell*, nothing in my life as a man or a beast has ever felt so damn good as this woman. This witch.

I could stay here all night like this, appreciating every detail.

The soothing sounds of her soft sighs and rapidly beating heart. The sweet-apple scent of her. Waves of black-and-silver hair spilling down her back. The scars of her past shimmering on her pale skin.

The beauty of all of it, every inch of her, every curve, every scar.

Mine...

But Westlyn is too eager, too needy to remain still. Her hips are already shifting again, her back arching, her whole body desperate for the release I've thus far denied her.

"Stop moving," I command, my palm flat on her back, holding her in place. "Now."

She stills beneath my hand, breath fogging the sleek mahogany finish of my desk, and I take one more moment to breathe her in. All of her.

My beautiful, insufferable, perfect little brat...

Ever so slowly, I begin moving my hips again, dragging out of her, then sinking back in, one inch at a time until her perfect pink flesh swallows my dark gray length, the contrasting colors of our skin shimmering where our bodies join. I lower my hands to her hips and grip her tightly, my tail working her clit with slow circles, her hair bouncing along her back with every thrust, faster and deeper, harder, thoughts and words fading away as we fuck and pant and devour and...

"Daddy," she breathes, her body fisting my cock as the orgasm crashes through her, and I tighten my grip on her hips and drive into her harder, once, twice, three more times and then...

Oh, fuck... That's it. Right fucking there, and I'm... I'm gone.

A roar rips through my chest, and I come inside her with the force of the waves breaking against the cliffs of my homeland, shuddering against her perfect skin until I forget about the dangers facing us both, forget about the curse, forget about the constant ache in my heart. I come until I'm utterly spent, until I can do nothing more but collapse on top of her and sigh, wishing this didn't have to be the last time.

It's the buzzing on my desk that saves us both—me, from losing myself to my own despair, and the little mortal from having to deal with another of my infamous mood swings.

"Looks like Klaiburn came through for us," I say, standing up and reading his text. "He was able to locate the box in your father's name—number 8164. The key is on his desk. Starting thirty minutes from now, the bank will be empty and security systems offline for unscheduled maintenance for exactly one hour."

I help her to her feet, my hands on her bare shoulders as she looks up at me with dazed, happy eyes.

They aren't the kind of eyes that speak to an intense physical connection. To a run of hot, filthy sex.

They're the kind of eyes that speak not of wild nights at all, but of slow, delicious mornings. Of breakfasts in bed. Of coffee gone cold over good conversation that bleeds into the afternoons, the evenings, and all the mornings that follow.

Mornings a gargoyle will never see.

Fresh pain twists my heart for all the things I can not have. All the things I can not give.

"Draegan," she whispers. "I—"

I press a finger to her lips, silencing her.

There are a thousand words I could say in this moment. Words I *should* say—the right and honorable ones. Or even the wrong but genuine ones.

But looking into her eyes now, I can't bring myself to say either.

Calling up my glamour and shoring up the walls around my heart, I say only, "Best clean up and find your clothing, Miss Avery. Time to go collect your inheritance."

CHAPTER THIRTY-FIVE

WESTLYN

The bank VP came through. Draegan and I found the bank empty, as promised, the key right where he said it'd be.

We found the safe deposit box. Together with the bank's key and mine, we opened it, revealing the long metal box inside, which now sits on a table in front of us in a so-called "privacy room" the size of closet, waiting to be opened.

Waiting to reveal its secrets.

A spark of excitement zips around my insides, but I can't even allow myself to enjoy this small victory.

My father left something important for me to find—something *so* important, he felt the need to hide it behind a series of clues so random and unlikely, I only figured them out by chance, with the help of my gargoyle A-team. Now, thanks to Draegan's connection at the bank, I'm about to get my hands on it. My so-called legacy, for better or worse.

I should be grateful. Ecstatic, even. We're one step closer to solving another piece of the puzzle.

But all I can think about is Draegan.

My mind is spinning. My heart is doing double time. And my pussy? I thought the poor thing had been through the wringer during that car ride the other night. But now? *Fuhgettaboutit.* After tonight's desktop dalliances? We are *never* going to recover.

Because all tonight's little escapade did was leave me desperately wanting more.

More kisses, more forbidden touches, more of those push-and-pull, Daddy Dom power games Draegan Caldwell is so, so good at...

Shit.

Things with that infuriating gargoyle have gone from *bad* bad (that first night in the manor), to *good* bad (all that oh-so-fun button-pushing), to so-fucking-hot-I-need-ice-in-my-pants bad (the drive home from the Ryker plant the other night), to I'm-pretty-sure-we-just-incinerated-my-panties-and-at-least-three-neighboring-counties bad (that whole desk-banging thing)... and he hasn't even acknowledged it.

Hasn't said a word about anything other than our bank mission since Klaiburn's ill-timed text came through.

Does he actually *regret* what happened between us tonight? Why? It's not like I'm asking him for a relationship or anything, perish the thought. And it's not like he didn't get off on all those filthy things he did to me, bent over the desk with my bare ass in the air, his tail rubbing my clit as he railed my pussy with his hot, massive, *perfectly* contoured—

"Miss *Avery*," Draegan barks from behind my chair. Even with him wearing his somewhat smaller human glamour, it's still way too close for comfort in this tiny room. And even with the glamour, yes, the jerk can still smell my desire. Desire that's already off the charts on a normal day around my gargoyles. Things on the horny home front got a lot more intense after I carved those fae runes and somehow unlocked my inner ho super-spirit. We're talking constant, regularly scheduled, time-release bursts of *give it to me, daddy* whenever Draegan's around.

Whenever *any* of my gargoyles are around.

And they all know it, too. Every damn time.

"If you don't mind focusing on the task at hand," he grits out, "we might actually make it back home before sunrise."

Stupid gargoyle super-senses.

"On it!" Ignoring the red-hot throb between my thighs, I give him the double-thumbs-up and grin, hoping the sudden burst of forced enthusiasm is enough to distract him from the *enthusiasm* going on between my thighs.

He doesn't respond.

I turn my attention back to the metal box. My hands tingle, everything in me dying to know what's inside.

Answers? Or more questions?

Either way, this is the moment we've all been waiting for...

So why the hell can't I bring myself to open it?

"I... I'm sorry," I whisper, tears stinging my eyes. "I don't know what's wrong with me. I'm totally freezing up."

"It's like a doorway, Miss Avery," Draegan says softly, surprising me with his sudden gentleness. "You've been given an opportunity to peek into another side of your father's life—one you've never had access to before. But once you open it, that's it. Whether the outcome is favorable or unfavorable doesn't matter. Either way, you won't be able to walk through that door again."

A tear slips down my cheek, and I nod. Because that's *exactly* it. My father and I barely spoke—not in recent years, anyway. This feels like a second chance.

One I'm not sure I actually want.

"Even after everything," I say, "I just... I don't want to be disappointed again."

His warm hand covers my shoulder, strong and comforting. "Whatever it is, we'll deal with it. Together."

Bolstered by the unexpected show of support, I take a deep breath and nod. "All right. Let's see what's behind this door, shall we?"

I flip open the lid, revealing...

Two small manilla envelopes. Nothing more, nothing less.

"And the plot thickens," Draegan says.

"Damn. I was really hoping for the fat stacks of cash and a deed to a beach house in the Hamptons."

"That sort of thing only happens in the movies."

"Gargoyles coming to life only happens in the movies too, remember?"

He laughs. "Touché."

"Okay then." I take another steadying breath and pick up the first envelope, pulling open the flap and dumping the contents into my hand.

It's some kind of oval-shaped jewel, amber shot through with veins of violet. It warms in my palm, giving off a faint glow that seems to be pulsing in time with my heartbeat.

"It's a fae protection amulet," Draegan says reverently. "Very rare, very powerful."

"Why would my father keep something like this hidden from me?"

"I'm not one to defend the man who tried to sell you off to a demon, but... Perhaps you're not the one he was keeping it from. I don't think he would've gone to the trouble of hiding the key behind your photo if he didn't want you to eventually find this."

I close my fingers around it. "It feels like my own heartbeat."

"That's the magic. It's connected with you, which means it was meant for you."

"There's no letter or anything..." I sigh. "It's beautiful, but none of this makes any sense."

"Try the other one. Maybe the two things go together somehow."

I set the jewel on the table and check the other envelope—just a tiny piece of plastic about the size of a postage stamp.

"An SSD card," Draegan says, plucking it from my palm for a closer look. "Any idea what's on it?"

"No clue." I check the envelope again, and the other one, and the metal box too, but this is all we've got. A fae amulet and a mysterious SSD card. There's no note, no indication of what the amulet is for or what the card contains. Bank account numbers? A will? The answers to the baffling mysteries of the life and times of Westlyn Avery?

"Does any of this look familiar?" Draegan asks, his hand curling protectively around the back of my neck. "The jewel... Have you ever seen it in photos? Or maybe he mentioned it in passing?"

"Nope. I've never seen it before. I feel like I would remember it if I had." I pick it up again, and the moment my fingers make contact, it restarts that slow, steady pulse. "Maybe it was my mother's?"

"That's possible, but unlikely. Protection amulets can be passed down, but only as collector's items. The magic inside them is keyed to one person, and one person only. It can't be changed or reset. If you're feeling its magic, your mother wouldn't have been able to."

"You're saying someone made this for me? A fae?"

"Or someone commissioned a fae to make it for you, yes. But it's definitely fae-crafted."

I take the SSD card back from him, holding it in my other hand. "This one *doesn't* have a heartbeat."

Draegan laughs. "I didn't think so. But it may have some answers."

"Assuming it's not password protected? Maybe. But if it is, I'm afraid we're out of luck. I barely knew my father—there's no way I can crack his password."

"Fortunately for us, we know someone who can." He gives me one more reassuring squeeze, and then we're off, sneaking back out of the empty bank with our loot stashed in Draegan's briefcase, his hand on my lower back, his eyes scanning every corner and every shadow for danger, just like always.

We get to the car without incident, where he promptly locks us in and zooms us out of the city.

He asks me if I'm cold, and turns on the heat when I nod.

He asks me if I'd like to pick the music, so I do.

He asks me if I'm feeling okay about what we found in the box, and reassures me that if anyone can figure out what's on that little card, Rook can.

But an hour into the drive back upstate, he still hasn't asked me about what happened between us in his office.

Not even to say it can't happen again, if that's how he feels.

It's like he just wants to pretend it never even happened at all.

I steal another glance at him across the dark space of the car, his profile striking in the glow of a passing streetlight. Strong, masculine jaw with just a hint of dark stubble. Black hair touched with gray, handsome and distinguished. Full, lush lips—lips I know from experience *excel* at delivering hot kisses and the kind of filthy whispers that make my toes curl.

He's wearing the glamour, but I can still picture the gargoyle beneath—the dark gray skin. The thick horns peeking out of that dark hair.

Everything about him says power. Strength. Loyalty.

And that's exactly who he is.

My first night at Blackmoor, Draegan Caldwell promised to keep me safe. Promised he wouldn't let my enemies touch me.

When he asked me what I wanted, I told him I wanted vengeance.

He promised me I could have it. I trust him to deliver.

In many ways, he already has. He and the other gargoyles, all of whom have sworn to protect me.

But now, after all these weeks with them, I want more than just vengeance. More than protection. More than solving the mystery of my existence and their curse and all the puzzles that connect them both.

I want a *life* with these gargoyles. A long, beautiful life filled with night breakfasts and library books and fireside chats and almond joy lattes and family dinners and wild, passionate nights that leave us tangled up and breathless and aching in all the best possible ways.

That was never part of the deal, though. And maybe it's too much to hope for anyway—just the silly wishes of a witch with no real magic. No real choice.

I close my eyes, barely keeping the tears at bay.

"Miss Avery? Are you all right?"

I feel his eyes on me. His scrutiny.

Just his protective instincts, I remind myself. *Just a gargoyle keeping his promises.*

I open my eyes and force a smile, flashing him another double-thumbs-up.

This time, it's not because I'm trying to distract him from my desire.

It's because I'm trying to protect the one thing Draegan *can't*, no matter how many promises he makes to keep me safe.

A thing I'm afraid I'm going to lose, once and for all, because all I want to do is give it to a man who doesn't even want it.

My heart.

"Miss Avery, whatever you're worried about, try not to let it trouble you." He turns to look at me again, and this time he cups my chin, his thumb stroking my cheek.

The tenderness in his eyes makes me want to open up to him. To tell him exactly what's troubling me, what I'm feeling, what I want, and let the proverbial chips fall where they may.

I turn toward the window, but he's still watching me. Still touching me, his every caress sending tiny shivers down my spine.

No. I spent too many years in hiding from my own life. Avoiding the real conversations. Avoiding my feelings.

Never again...

I turn and face him once more.

Our gazes lock, fierce and fiery.

I take a deep breath. Open my mouth to tell him everything—how I feel. How I know it's not part of our deal, but I want it anyway. How I suspect, deep down, they want it too. Even Draegan.

But before I can put even *one* of those thoughts into words, there's a blinding light and a horrible screech and all I can say is, "Drae! Look out!"

Metal on metal.

Shattering glass.

Spinning, spinning, spinning.

Darkness.

They say in the moment before your death, time slows to a crawl, and your life flashes before your eyes.

But in my moment, when the world goes still and Death is breathing on the back of my neck, here's what I've got:

The taste of blood in my mouth.

The smell of burning rubber and spilled gasoline.

Flames licking at my skin, desperate for a taste.

And a lone voice echoing through my head.

Don't fear, little one. Everything is unfolding exactly as it should be...

Thank you so much for reading Wicked Awakening!

As the war on their enemies heats up and the shadow mage conspiracy against Westlyn slowly comes to light, what terrors await our fearless witch and her four possessive gargoyles?

Find out what happens next in **Wicked Devouring, book three of the Claimed by Gargoyles series.**

But first... have you grabbed your free bonus novella, A Gargoyle Obsessed, featuring that hot, devoted psycho Jude Hendrix?

Sign up for my newsletter and you'll receive your copy. This story takes place the night Jude first meets his sweet little scarecrow in the park, and it can't be found anywhere else—it's an exclusive gift just for my subscribers. And it's available in ebook AND audio!

Can't see the link? Visit SarahPiperBooks.com/jude to claim your copy.

Are you a member of our private Facebook group, <u>Sarah Piper's Sassy Witches?</u> Pop in for sneak peeks, cover reveals, exclusive giveaways, book chats, group therapy to deal with these killer cliffhangers, and plenty of complete randomness from your fellow fans! We'd love to see you there.

XOXO,
Sarah

group at Sarah Piper's Sassy Witches! If you're sassy, or if you need a little *more* sass in your life, or if you need more Dean Winchester gifs in your life (who doesn't?), come hang out!